—

THE ALL NEW!
BATMAN
THE BRAVE AND THE BOLD

WITHDRAWN

STONE ARCH BOOKS
a capstone imprint

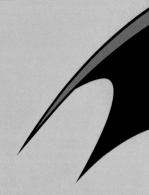

STONE ARCH BOOKS™

Published in 2015 by Stone Arch Books
A Capstone Imprint
1710 Roe Crest Drive
North Mankato, MN 56003
www.capstonepub.com

Originally published by DC Comics in the U.S. in single magazine form as The All-New Batman: The Brave and the Bold #4.
Original U.S. Editors: Scott Peterson and Jim Chadwick

DC Comics
1700 Broadway, New York, NY 10019
A Warner Bros. Entertainment Company

Library of Congress Cataloging-in-Publication Data

Fisch, Sholly, author.
The bride and the bold / Sholly Fisch, writer ; Rick Burchett, penciler ; Dan Davis, inker ; Gabe Eltaeb, colorist.
pages cm. -- (The all-new Batman: the brave and the bold ; 4)
"Originally published by DC Comics in the U.S. in single magazine form as The All-New Batman: The Brave and the Bold #4."
"Batman created by Bob Kane."
Summary: It is Valentine's Day, and you are invited to the wedding of Batman and Wonder Woman.
ISBN 978-1-4342-9661-0 (library binding)
1. Batman (Fictitious character)--Comic books, strips, etc. 2. Batman (Fictitious character)--Juvenile fiction. 3. Wonder Woman (Fictitious character)--Comic books, strips, etc. 4. Wonder Woman (Fictitious character)--Juvenile fiction. 5. Superheroes--Comic books, strips, etc. 6. Superheroes--Juvenile fiction. 7. Weddings--Comic books, strips, etc. 8. Weddings--Juvenile fiction. 9. Graphic novels. [1. Graphic novels. 2. Superheroes--Fiction. 3. Weddings--Fiction.] I. Burchett, Rick, illustrator. II. Kane, Bob, creator. III. Title.

PZ7.7.F57Br 2015
741.5'973--dc23

2014028253

STONE ARCH BOOKS
Ashley C. Andersen Zantop Publisher
Michael Dahl Editorial Director
Eliza Leahy Editor
Heather Kindseth Creative Director
Bob Lentz Art Director
Peggie Carley Designer
Katy LaVigne Production Specialist

Printed in China by Nordica.
0914/CA21401510
092014 008470NORDS15

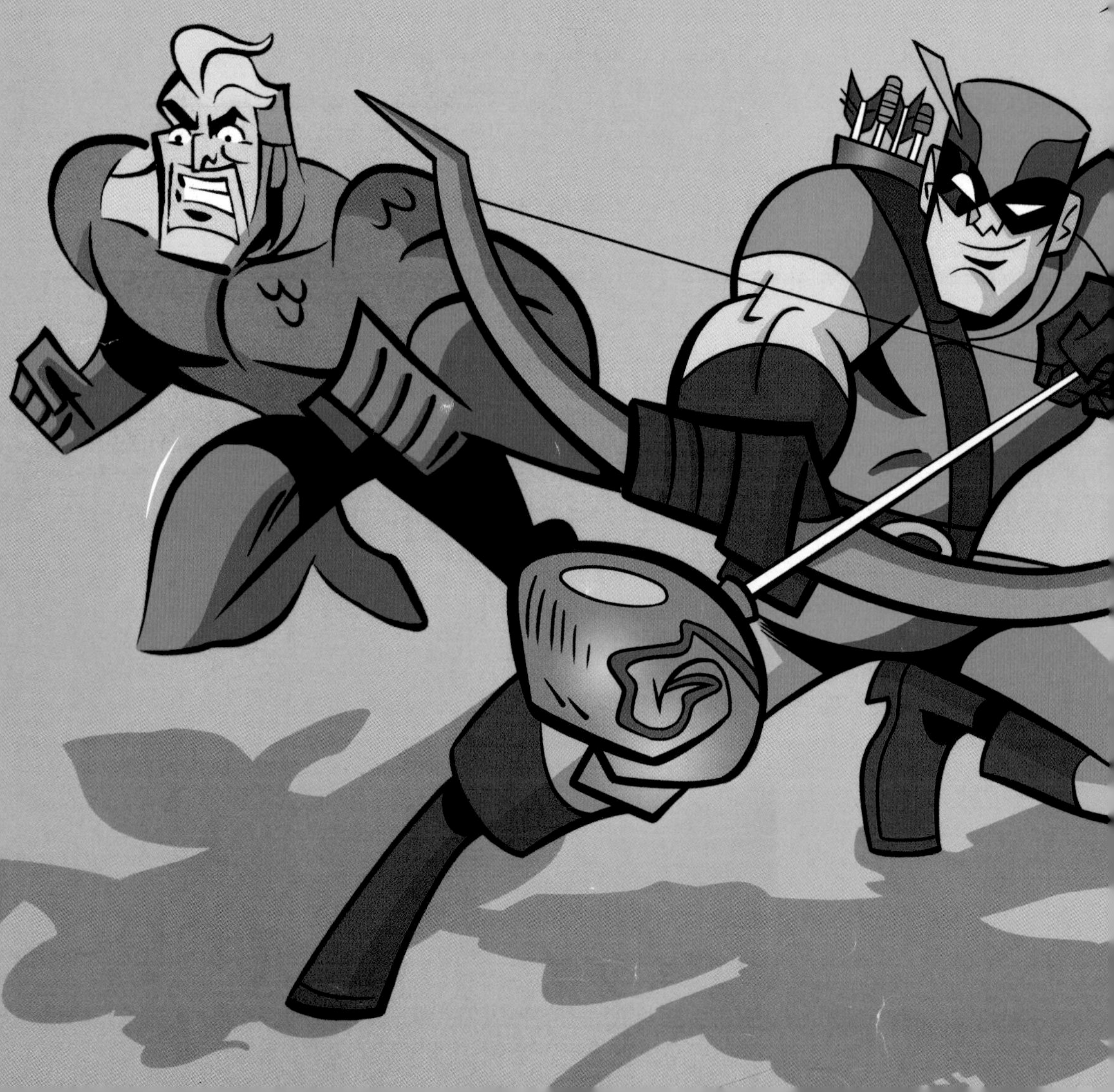

THE ALL NEW!

BATMAN

THE BRAVE AND THE BOLD

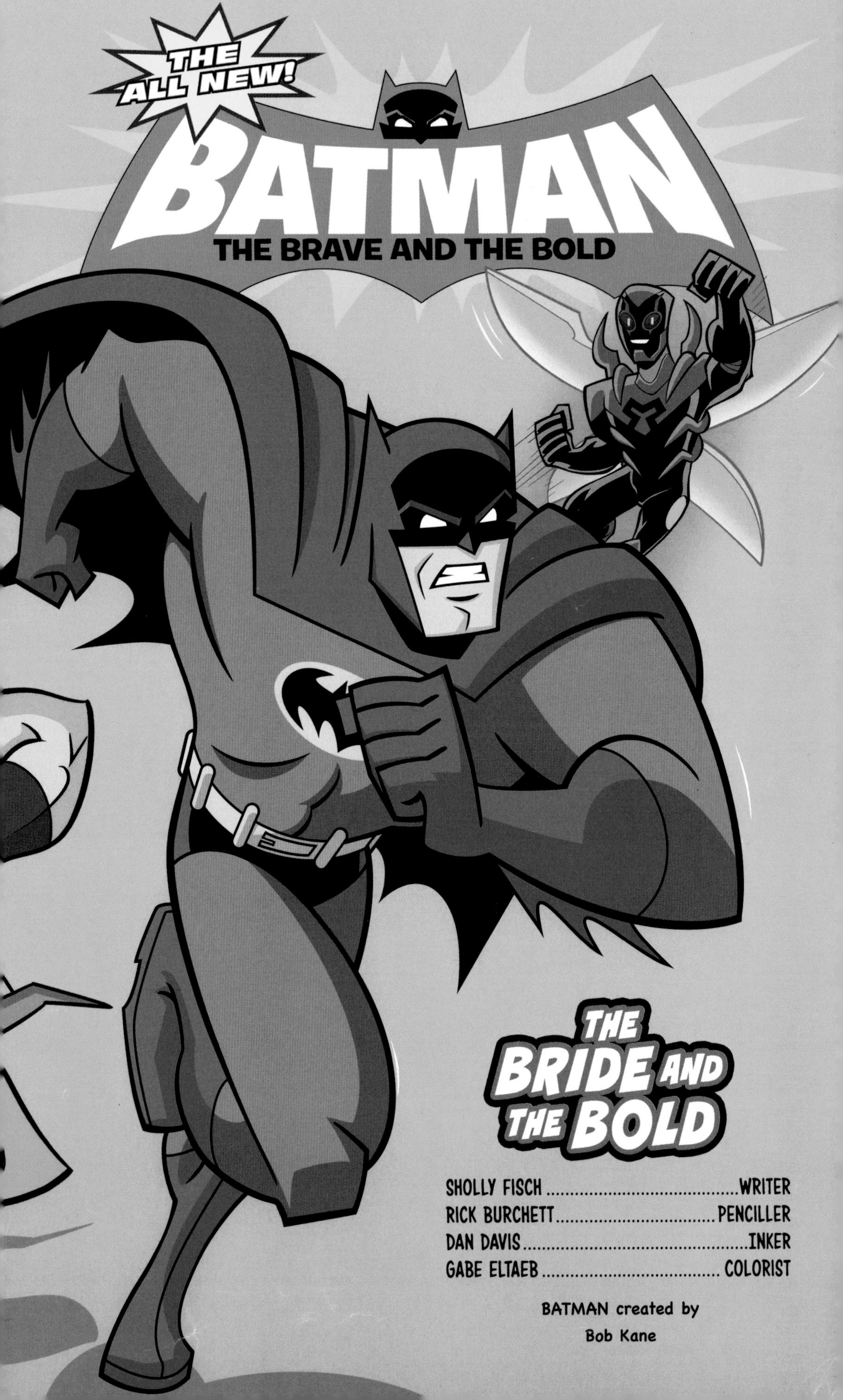

THE BRIDE AND THE BOLD

SHOLLY FISCH ....WRITER
RICK BURCHETT.................................PENCILLER
DAN DAVIS..INKER
GABE ELTAEB .... COLORIST

BATMAN created by
Bob Kane

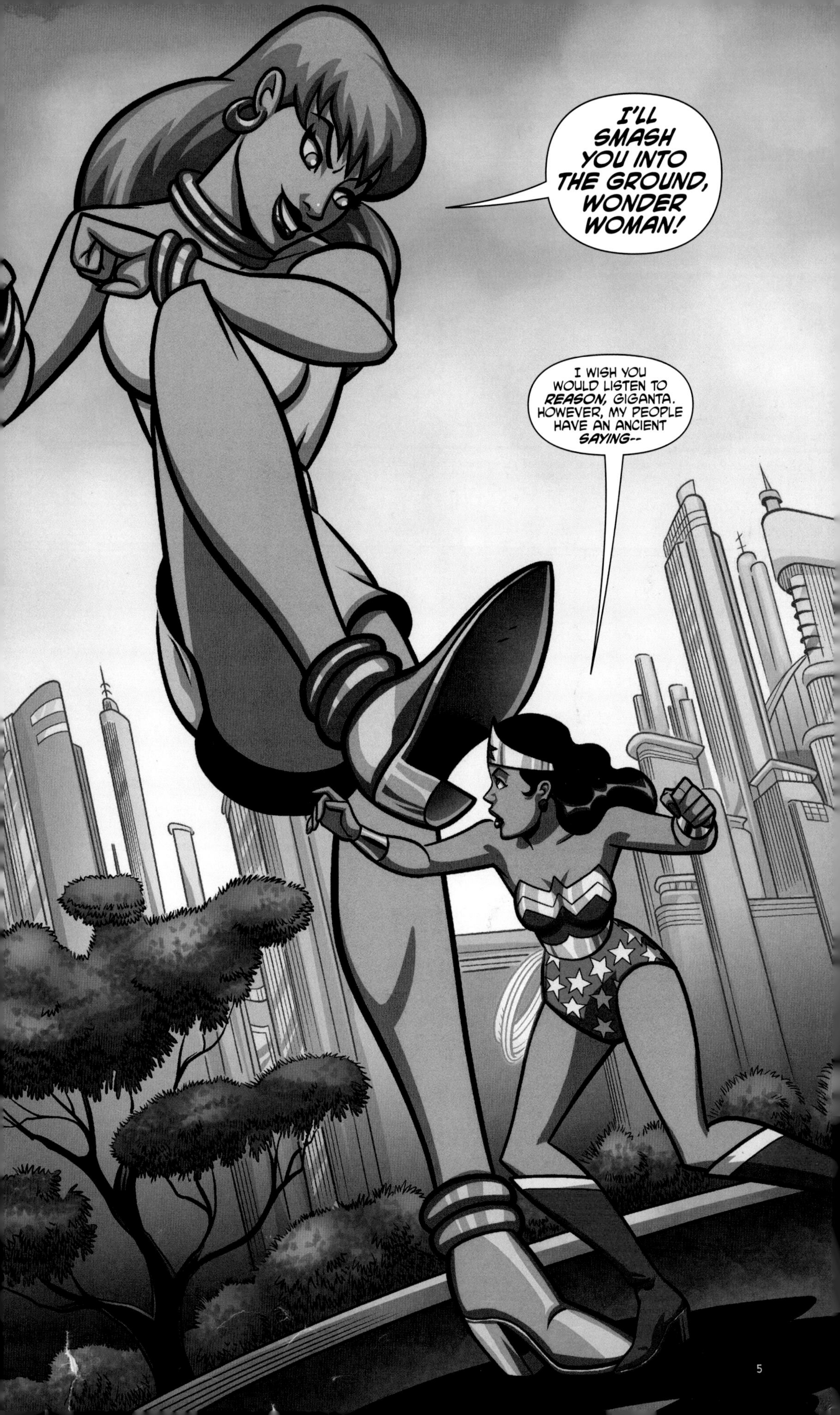
I'LL SMASH YOU INTO THE GROUND, WONDER WOMAN!
I WISH YOU WOULD LISTEN TO REASON, GIGANTA. HOWEVER, MY PEOPLE HAVE AN ANCIENT SAYING--

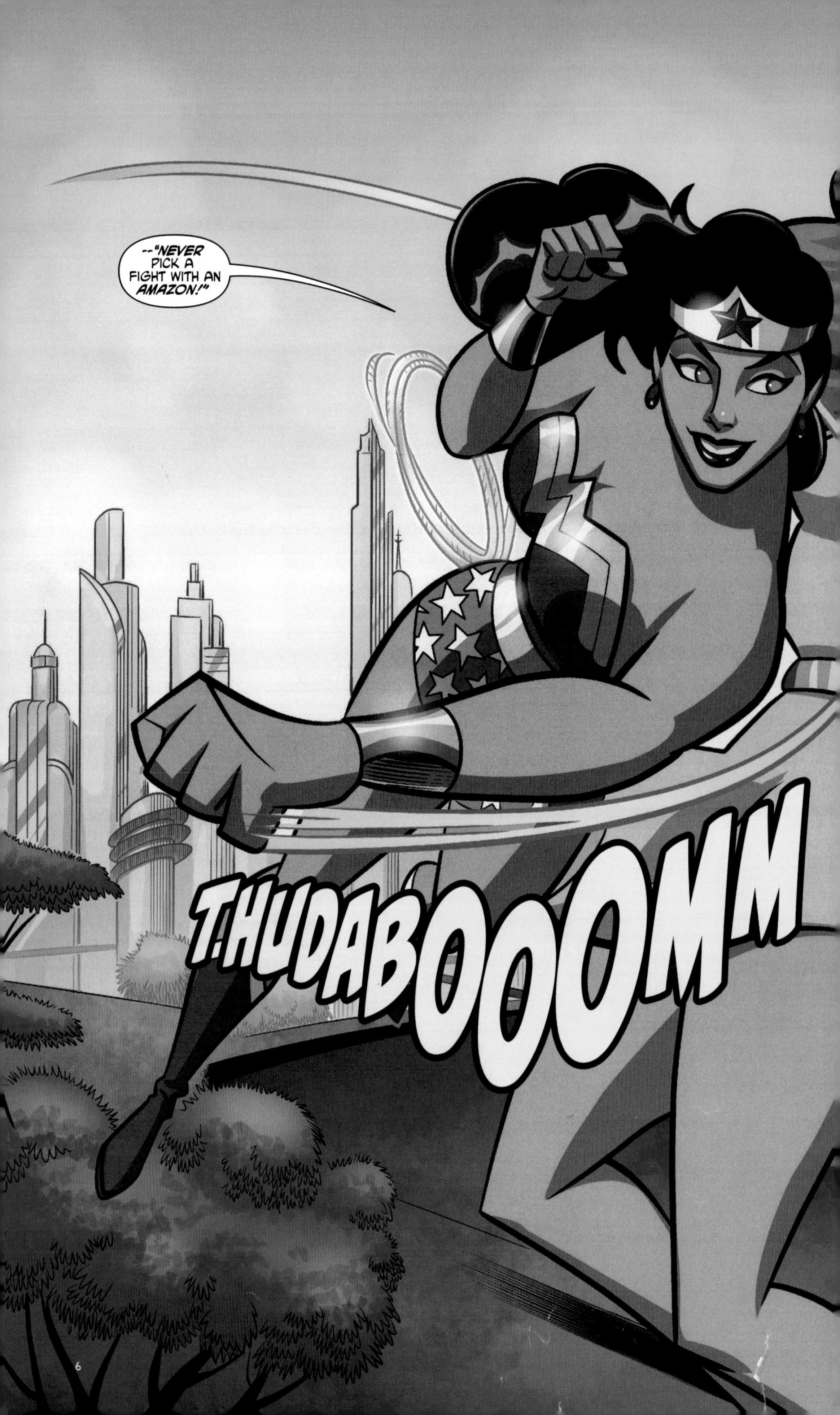
--"NEVER PICK A FIGHT WITH AN AMAZON!"
THUDABOOOMM

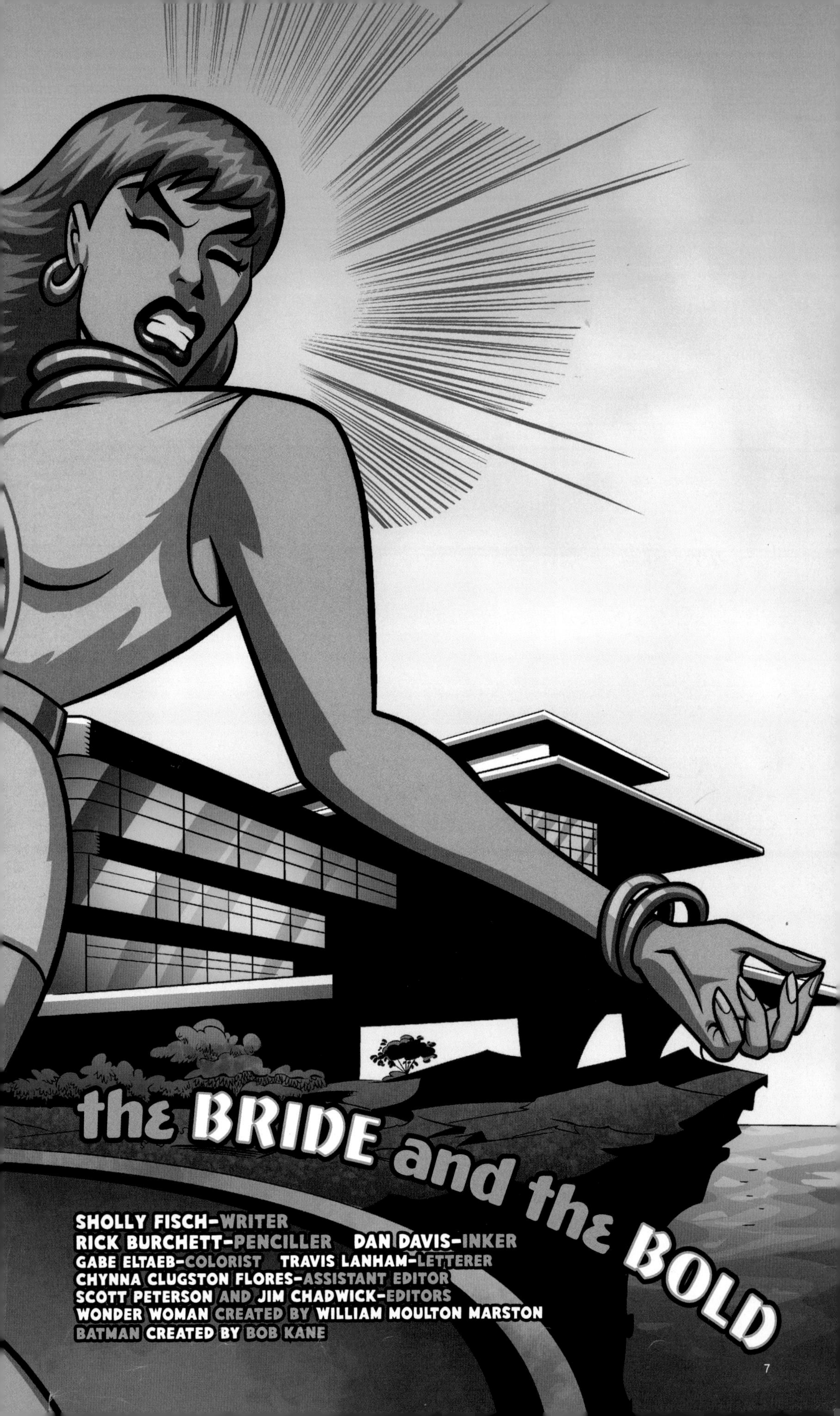

the BRIDE and the BOLD
SHOLLY FISCH-WRITER
RICK BURCHETT-PENCILLER DAN DAVIS-INKER
GABE ELTAEB-COLORIST TRAVIS LANHAM-LETTERER
CHYNNA CLUGSTON FLORES-ASSISTANT EDITOR
SCOTT PETERSON AND JIM CHADWICK-EDITORS
WONDER WOMAN CREATED BY WILLIAM MOULTON MARSTON
BATMAN CREATED BY BOB KANE

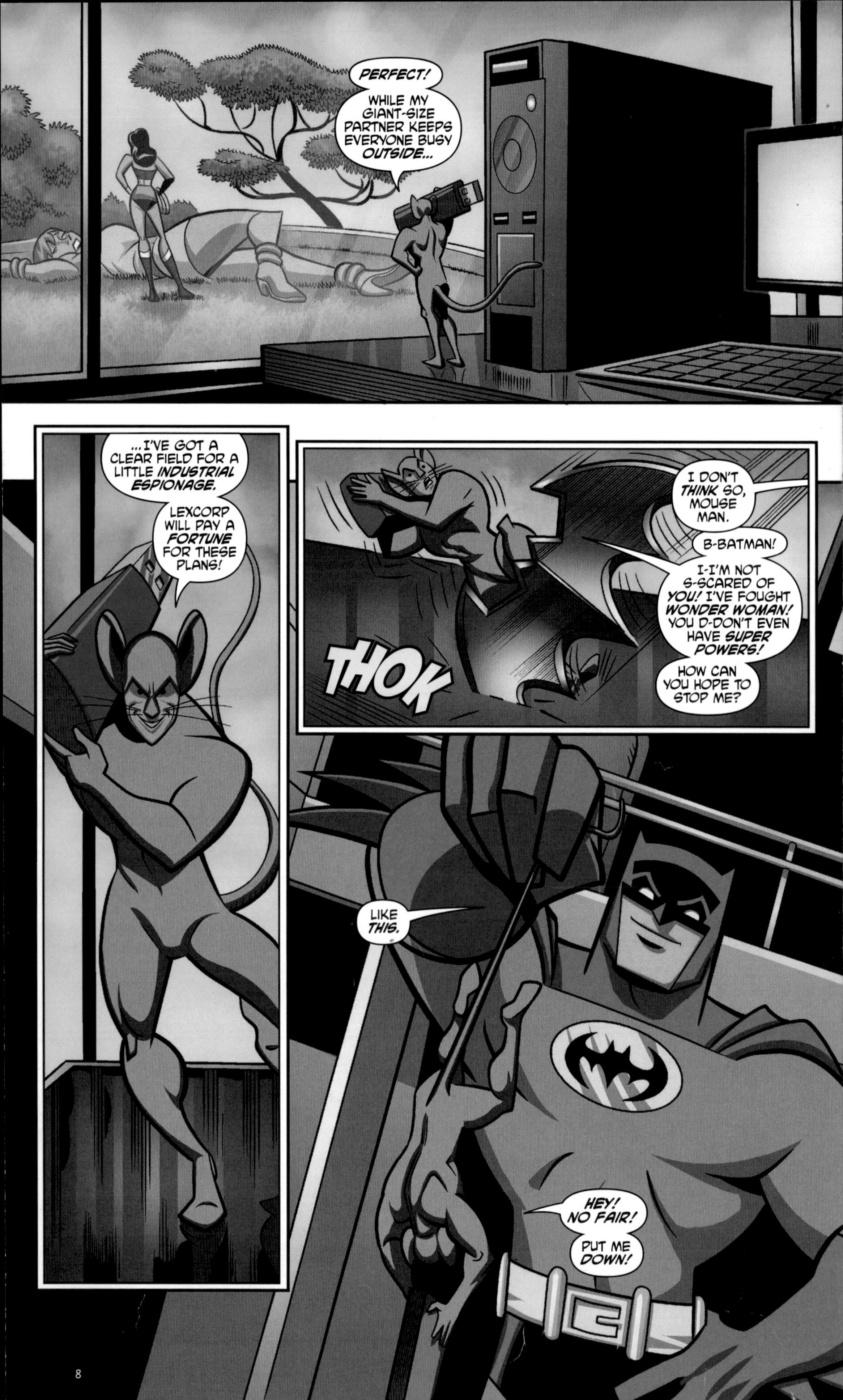

PERFECT!
WHILE MY GIANT-SIZE PARTNER KEEPS EVERYONE BUSY OUTSIDE...
...I'VE GOT A CLEAR FIELD FOR A LITTLE INDUSTRIAL ESPIONAGE.
LEXCORP WILL PAY A FORTUNE FOR THESE PLANS!
I DON'T THINK SO, MOUSE MAN.
B-BATMAN!
I-I'M NOT S-SCARED OF YOU! I'VE FOUGHT WONDER WOMAN! YOU D-DON'T EVEN HAVE SUPER POWERS!
HOW CAN YOU HOPE TO STOP ME?
THOK
LIKE THIS.
HEY! NO FAIR!
PUT ME DOWN!

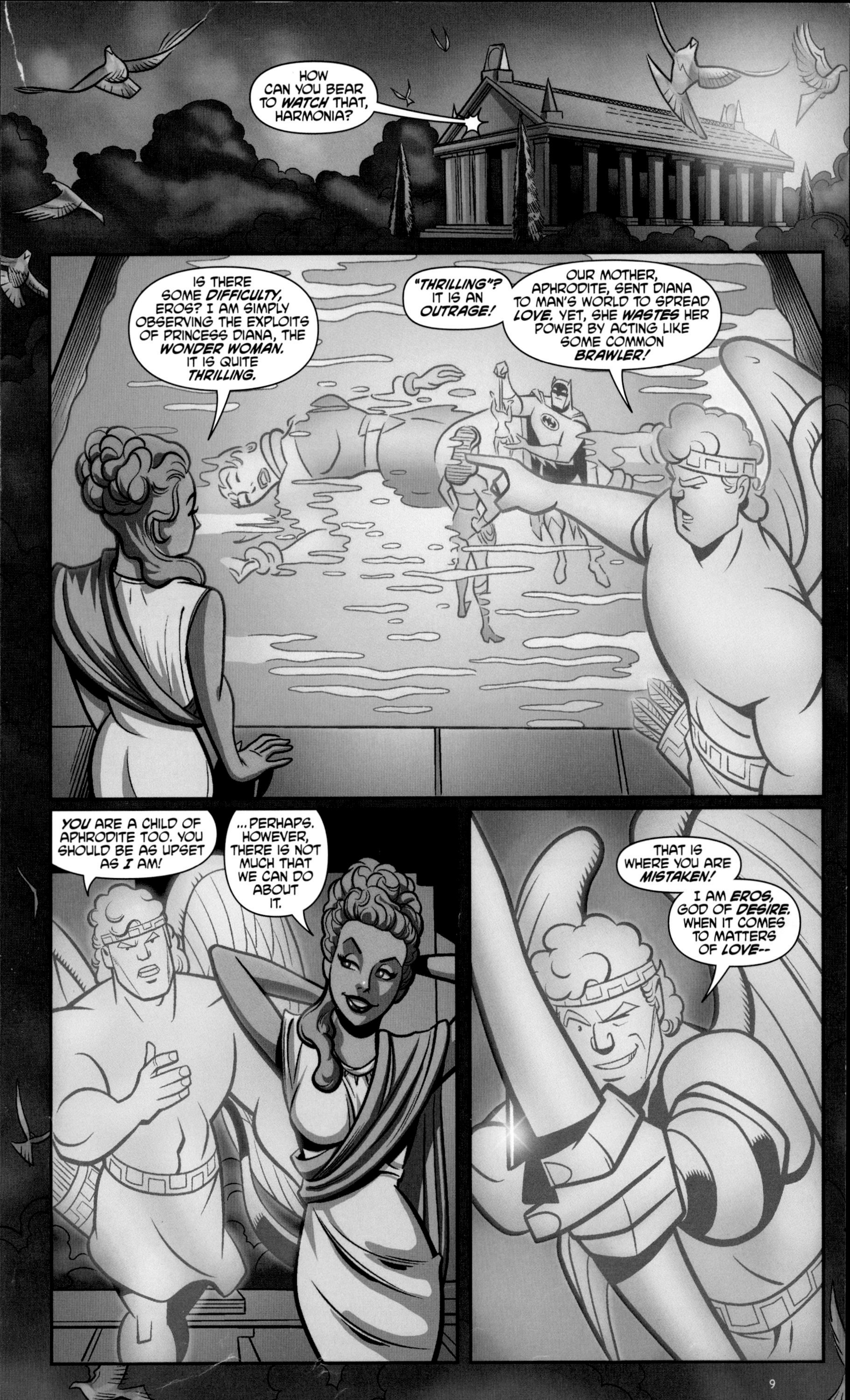

HOW CAN YOU BEAR TO *WATCH* THAT, HARMONIA?
IS THERE SOME *DIFFICULTY,* EROS? I AM SIMPLY OBSERVING THE EXPLOITS OF PRINCESS DIANA, THE *WONDER WOMAN.* IT IS QUITE *THRILLING.*
"THRILLING"? IT IS AN *OUTRAGE!*
OUR MOTHER, APHRODITE, SENT DIANA TO MAN'S WORLD TO SPREAD *LOVE.* YET, SHE *WASTES* HER POWER BY ACTING LIKE SOME COMMON *BRAWLER!*
YOU ARE A CHILD OF APHRODITE TOO. YOU SHOULD BE AS UPSET AS *I* AM!
...PERHAPS. HOWEVER, THERE IS NOT MUCH THAT WE CAN DO ABOUT IT.
THAT IS WHERE YOU ARE *MISTAKEN!*
I AM *EROS,* GOD OF *DESIRE.* WHEN IT COMES TO MATTERS OF *LOVE--*

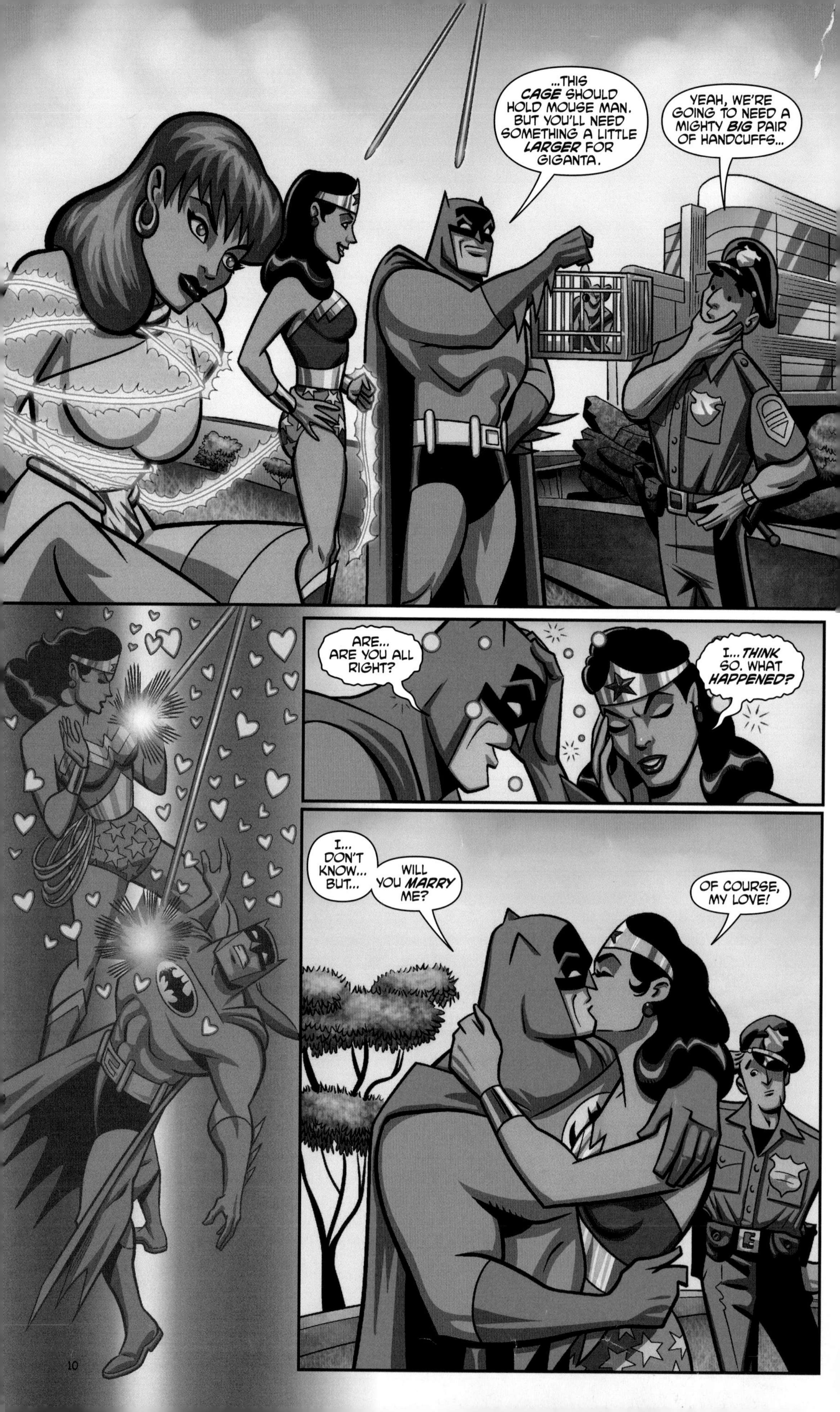
...THIS CAGE SHOULD HOLD MOUSE MAN. BUT YOU'LL NEED SOMETHING A LITTLE LARGER FOR GIGANTA.
YEAH, WE'RE GOING TO NEED A MIGHTY BIG PAIR OF HANDCUFFS...
ARE... ARE YOU ALL RIGHT?
I... THINK SO. WHAT HAPPENED?
I... DON'T KNOW... BUT...
WILL YOU MARRY ME?
OF COURSE, MY LOVE!

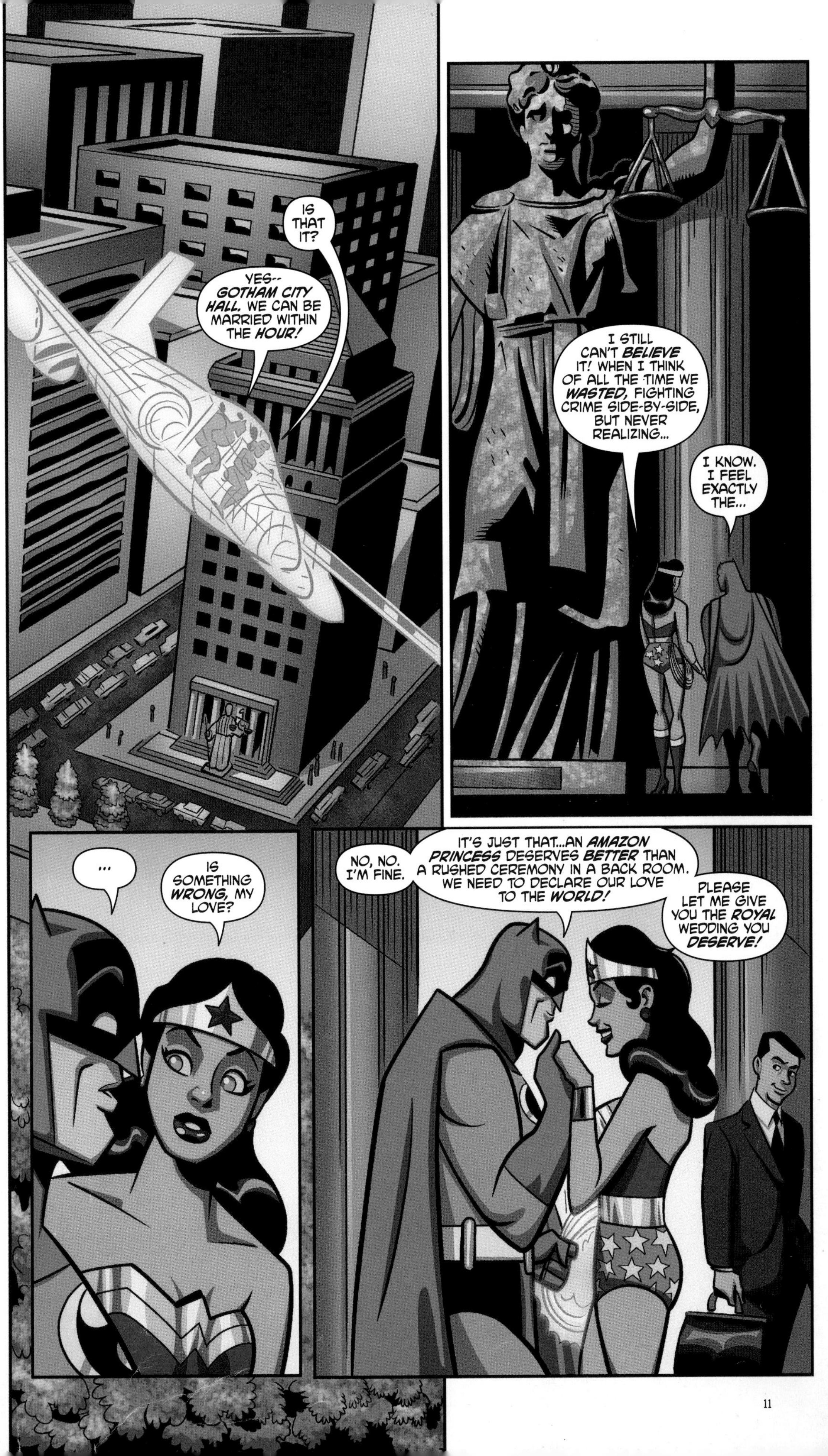
IS THAT IT?
YES-- GOTHAM CITY HALL. WE CAN BE MARRIED WITHIN THE HOUR!
I STILL CAN'T BELIEVE IT! WHEN I THINK OF ALL THE TIME WE WASTED, FIGHTING CRIME SIDE-BY-SIDE, BUT NEVER REALIZING...
I KNOW. I FEEL EXACTLY THE...
...
IS SOMETHING WRONG, MY LOVE?
NO, NO. I'M FINE.
IT'S JUST THAT...AN AMAZON PRINCESS DESERVES BETTER THAN A RUSHED CEREMONY IN A BACK ROOM. WE NEED TO DECLARE OUR LOVE TO THE WORLD!
PLEASE LET ME GIVE YOU THE ROYAL WEDDING YOU DESERVE!

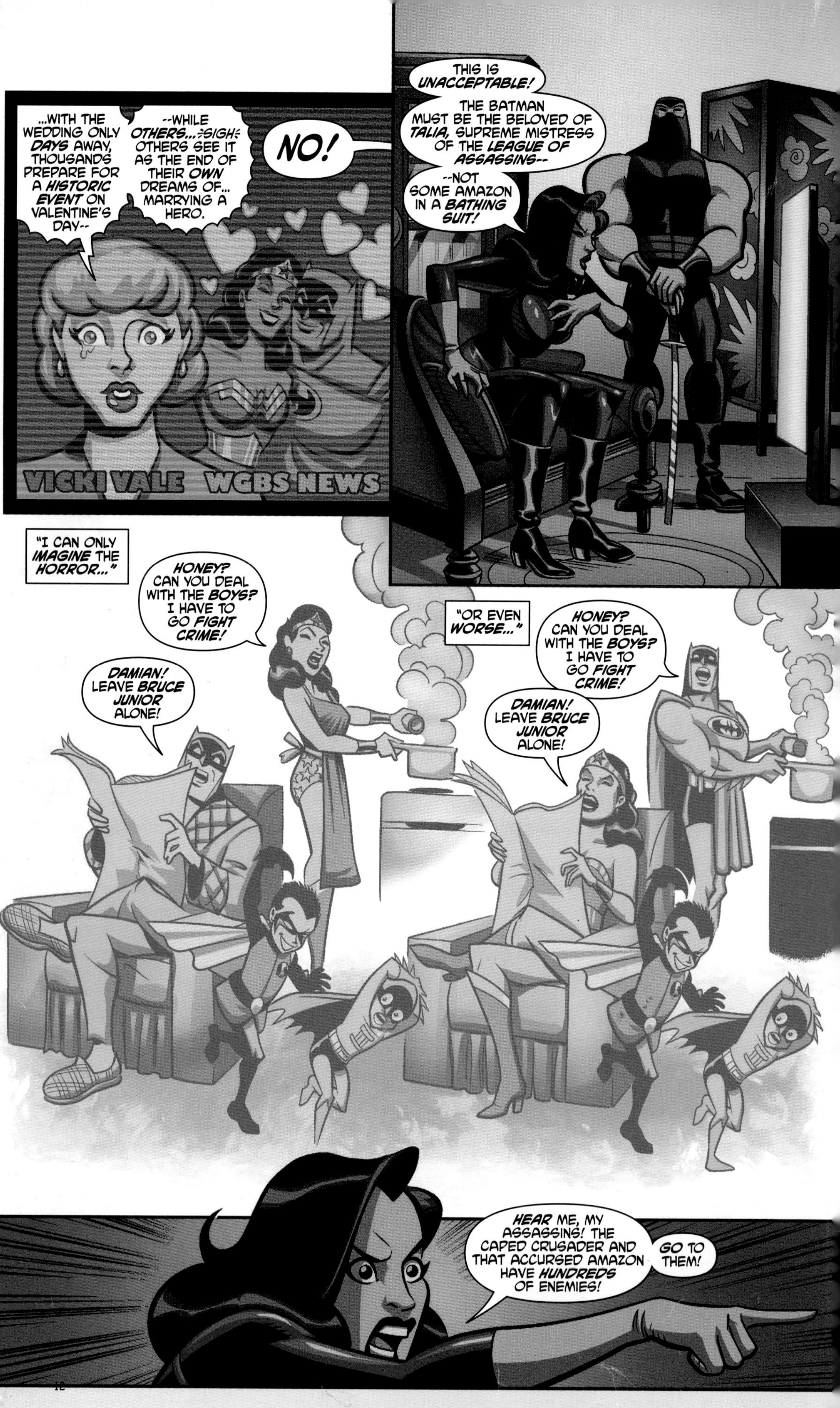
...WITH THE WEDDING ONLY DAYS AWAY, THOUSANDS PREPARE FOR A HISTORIC EVENT ON VALENTINE'S DAY--
--WHILE OTHERS... SIGH OTHERS SEE IT AS THE END OF THEIR OWN DREAMS OF... MARRYING A HERO.
NO!
VICKI VALE WGBS NEWS
THIS IS UNACCEPTABLE!
THE BATMAN MUST BE THE BELOVED OF TALIA, SUPREME MISTRESS OF THE LEAGUE OF ASSASSINS--
--NOT SOME AMAZON IN A BATHING SUIT!
"I CAN ONLY IMAGINE THE HORROR..."
HONEY? CAN YOU DEAL WITH THE BOYS? I HAVE TO GO FIGHT CRIME!
DAMIAN! LEAVE BRUCE JUNIOR ALONE!
"OR EVEN WORSE..."
HONEY? CAN YOU DEAL WITH THE BOYS? I HAVE TO GO FIGHT CRIME!
DAMIAN! LEAVE BRUCE JUNIOR ALONE!
HEAR ME, MY ASSASSINS! THE CAPED CRUSADER AND THAT ACCURSED AMAZON HAVE HUNDREDS OF ENEMIES!
GO TO THEM!

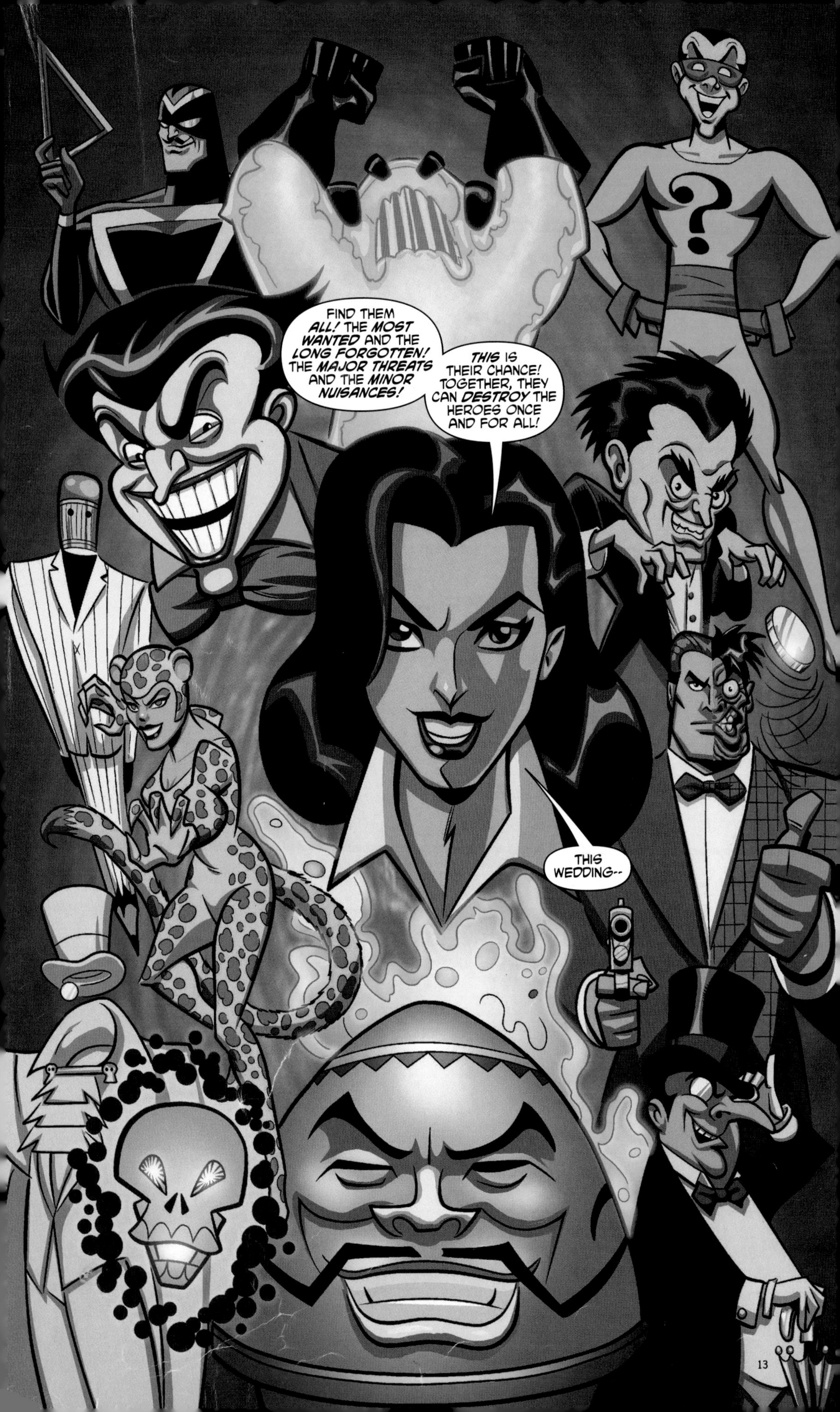
FIND THEM ALL! THE MOST WANTED AND THE LONG FORGOTTEN! THE MAJOR THREATS AND THE MINOR NUISANCES!
THIS IS THEIR CHANCE! TOGETHER, THEY CAN DESTROY THE HEROES ONCE AND FOR ALL!
THIS WEDDING--

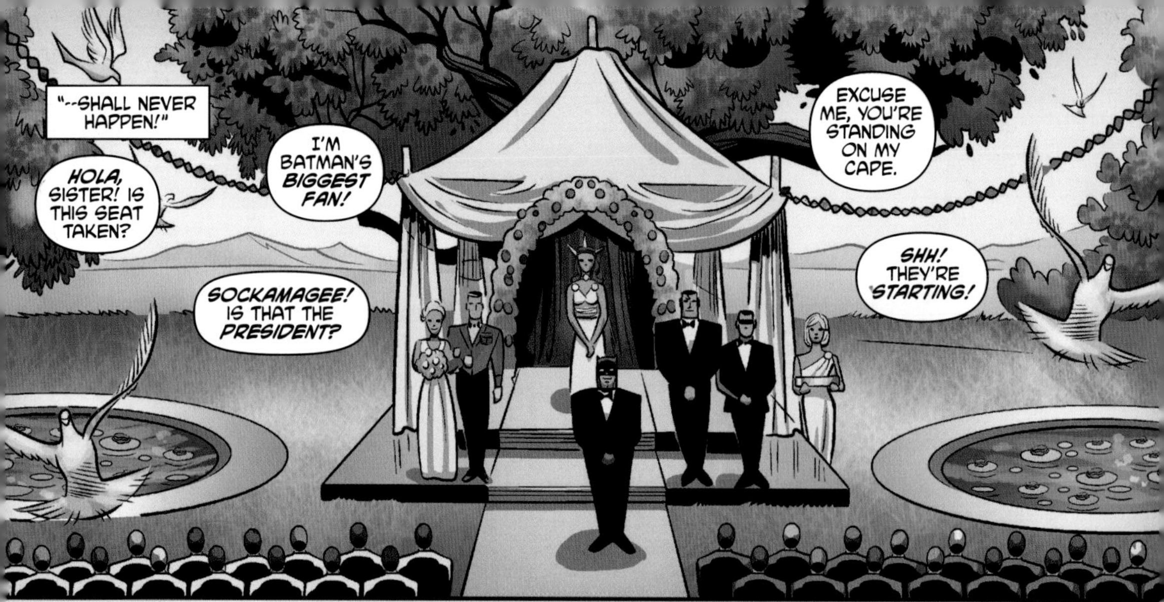
"--SHALL NEVER HAPPEN!"
HOLA, SISTER! IS THIS SEAT TAKEN?
I'M BATMAN'S BIGGEST FAN!
SOCKAMAGEE! IS THAT THE PRESIDENT?
EXCUSE ME, YOU'RE STANDING ON MY CAPE.
SHH! THEY'RE STARTING!

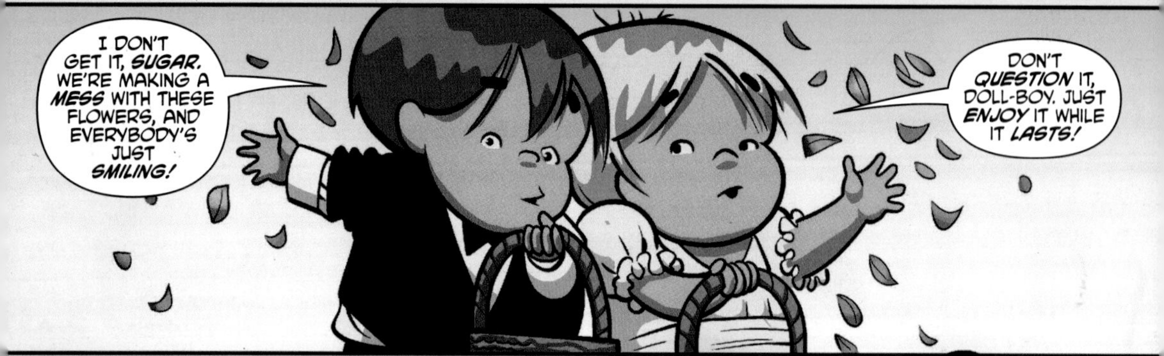
I DON'T GET IT, SUGAR. WE'RE MAKING A MESS WITH THESE FLOWERS, AND EVERYBODY'S JUST SMILING!
DON'T QUESTION IT, DOLL-BOY. JUST ENJOY IT WHILE IT LASTS!

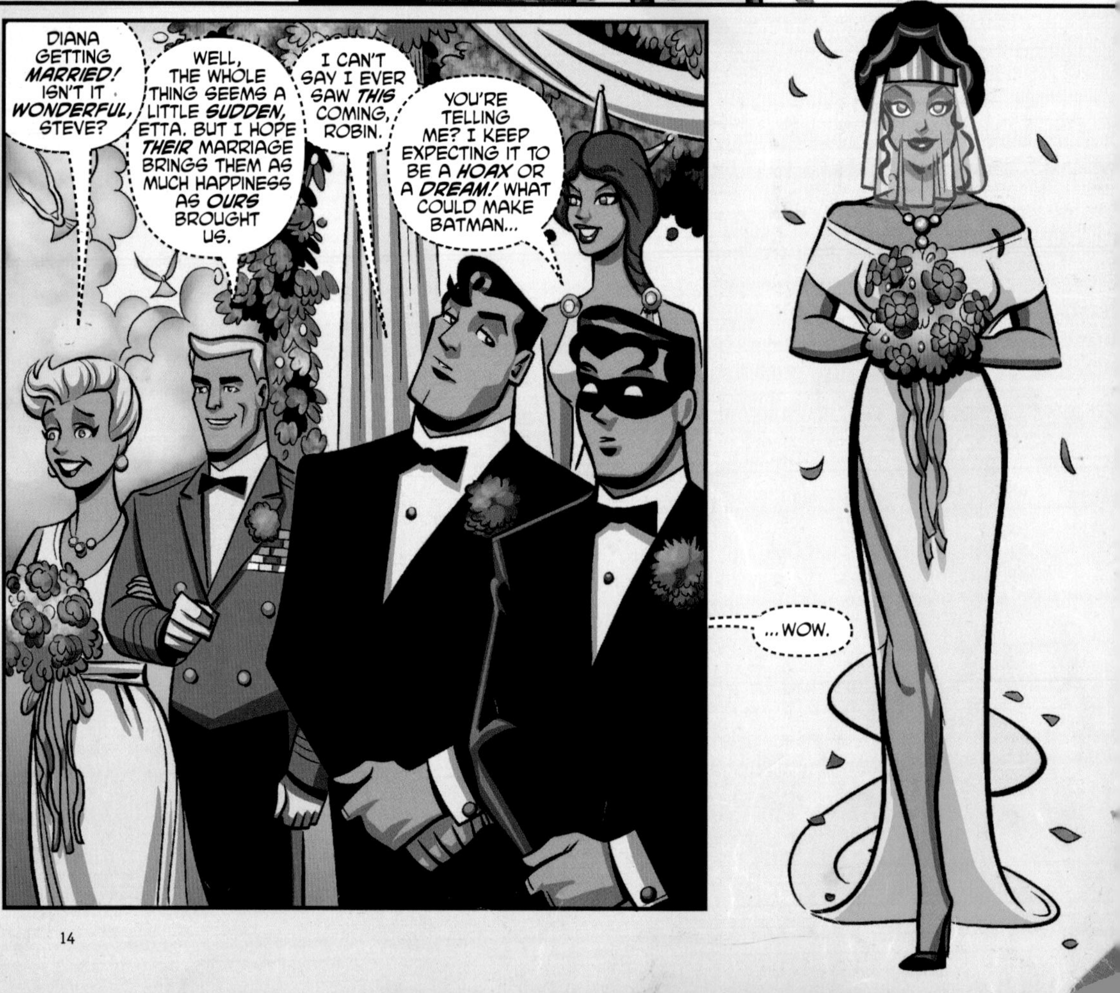
DIANA GETTING MARRIED! ISN'T IT WONDERFUL, STEVE?
WELL, THE WHOLE THING SEEMS A LITTLE SUDDEN, ETTA. BUT I HOPE THEIR MARRIAGE BRINGS THEM AS MUCH HAPPINESS AS OURS BROUGHT US.
I CAN'T SAY I EVER SAW THIS COMING, ROBIN.
YOU'RE TELLING ME? I KEEP EXPECTING IT TO BE A HOAX OR A DREAM! WHAT COULD MAKE BATMAN...
...WOW.

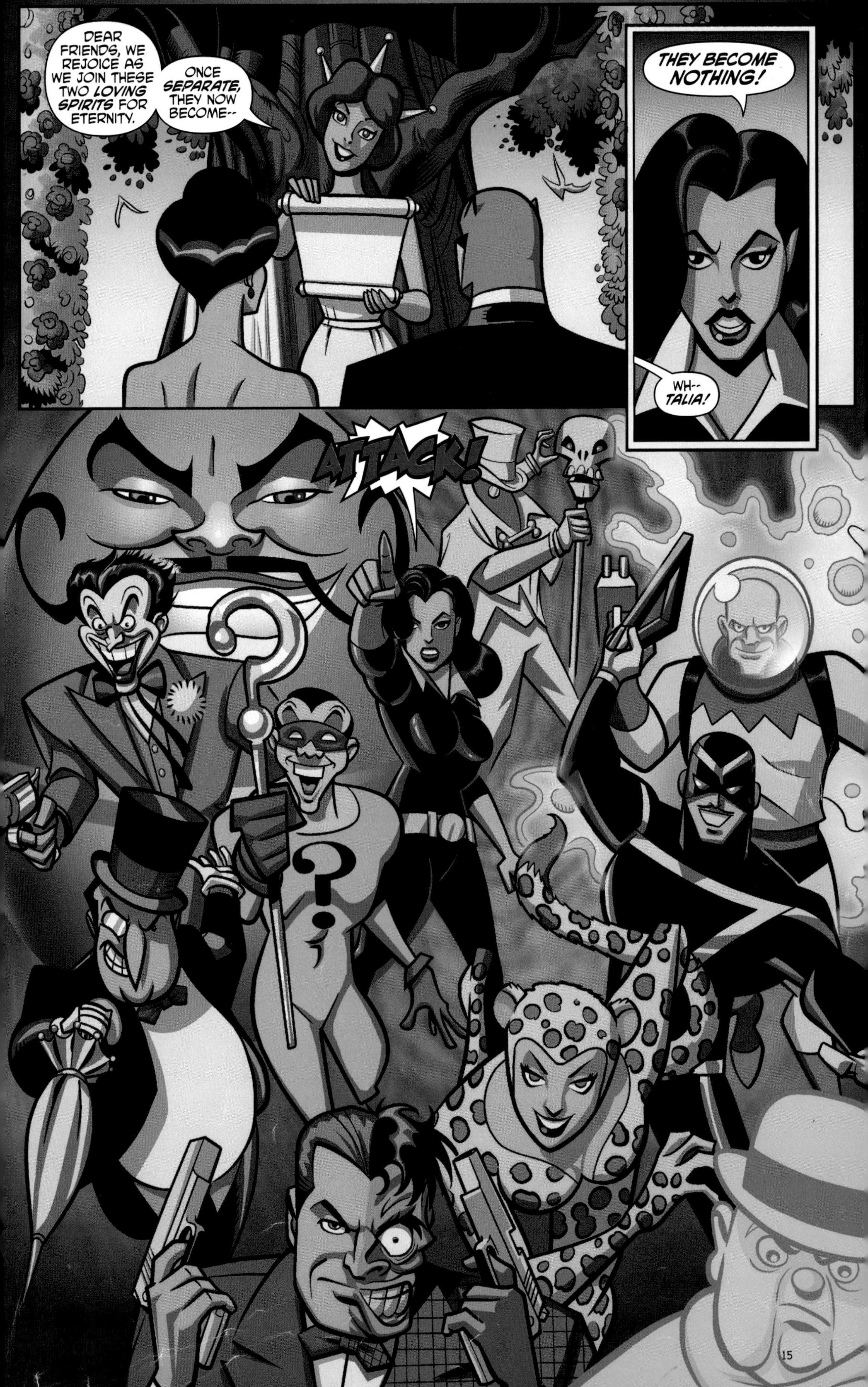
DEAR FRIENDS, WE REJOICE AS WE JOIN THESE TWO LOVING SPIRITS FOR ETERNITY.
ONCE SEPARATE, THEY NOW BECOME--
THEY BECOME NOTHING!
WH-- TALIA!
ATTACK!

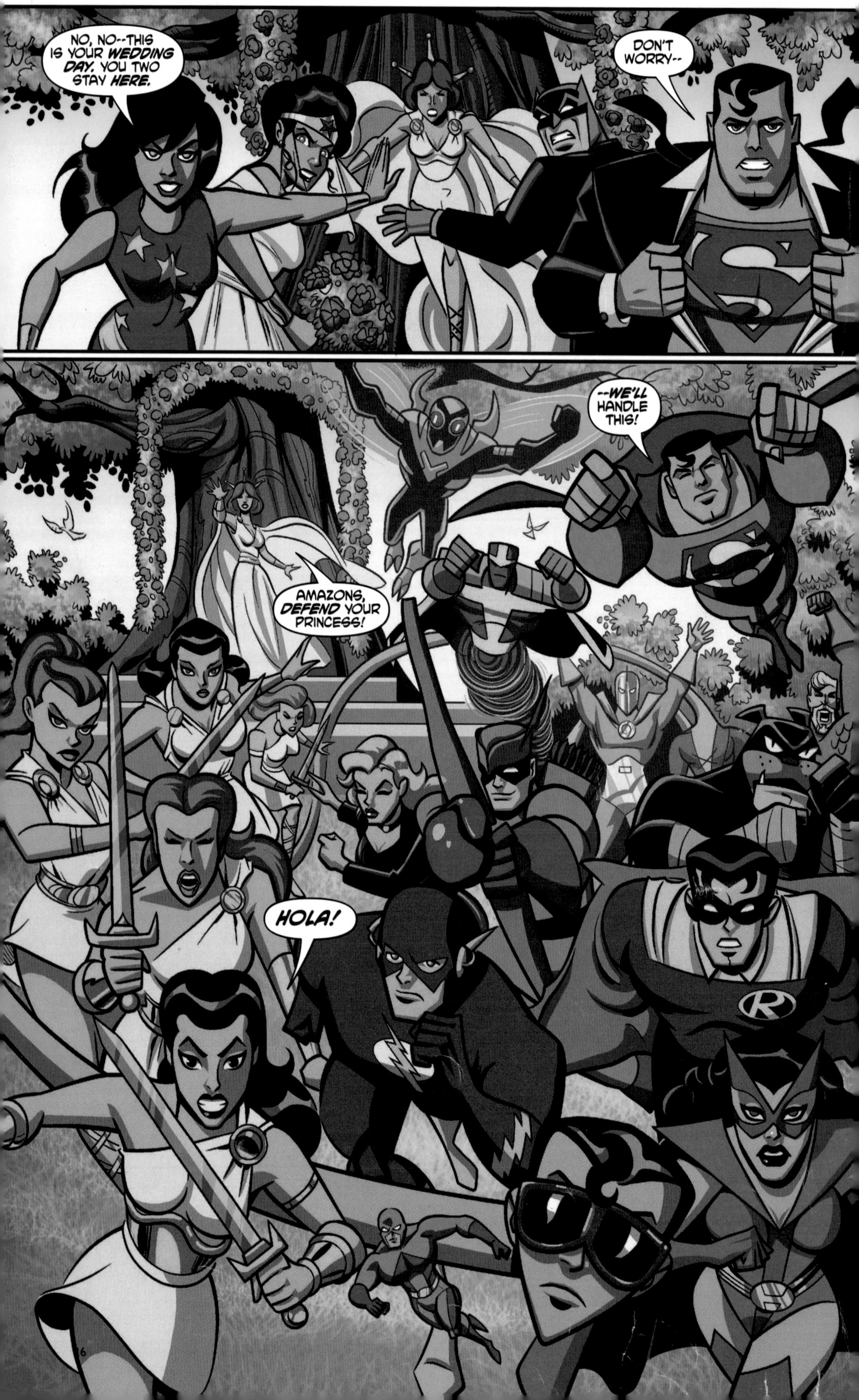
NO, NO--THIS IS YOUR WEDDING DAY. YOU TWO STAY HERE.
DON'T WORRY--
--WE'LL HANDLE THIS!
AMAZONS, DEFEND YOUR PRINCESS!
HOLA!

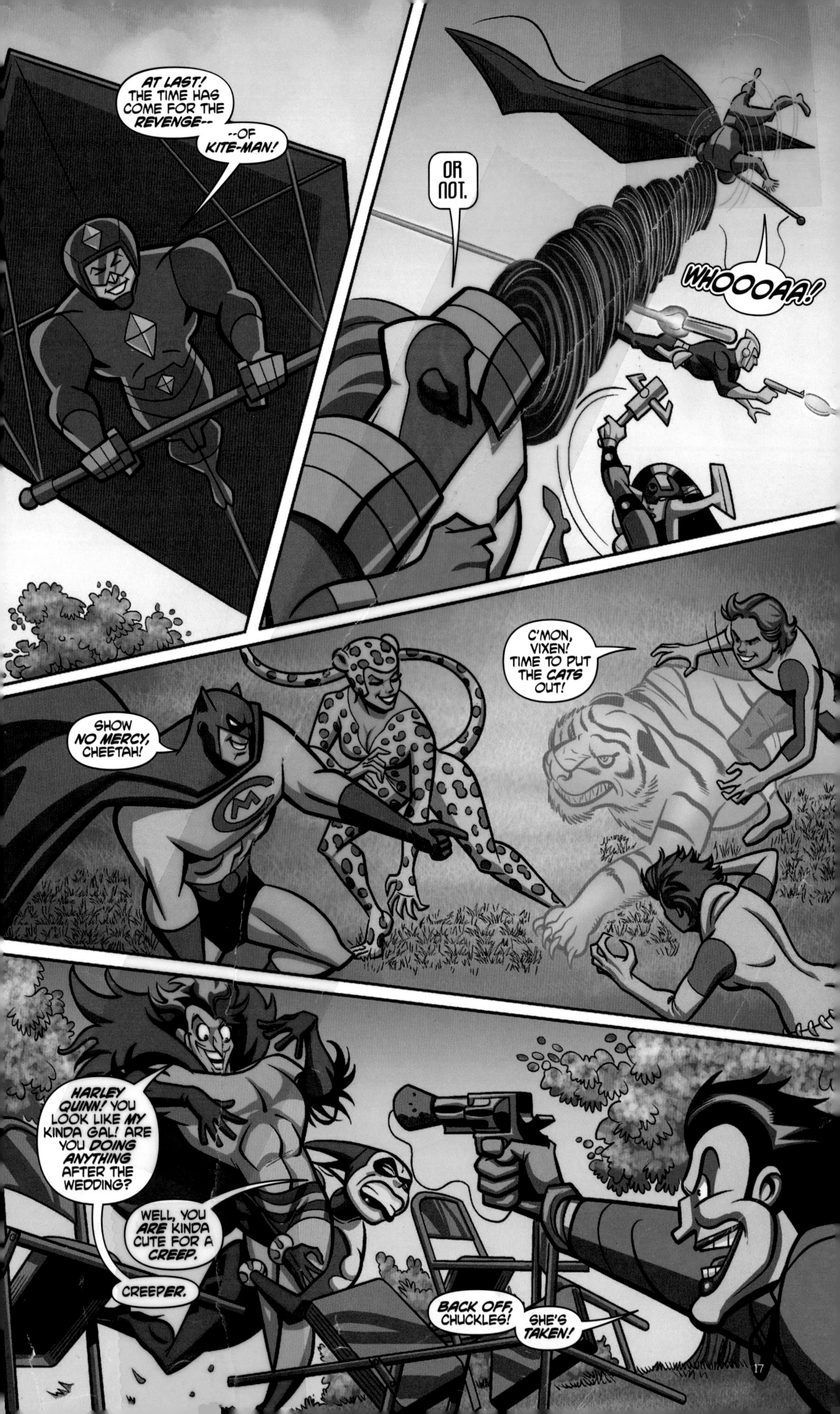

AT LAST! THE TIME HAS COME FOR THE REVENGE--
--OF KITE-MAN!
OR NOT.
WHOOOAA!
SHOW NO MERCY, CHEETAH!
C'MON, VIXEN! TIME TO PUT THE CATS OUT!
HARLEY QUINN! YOU LOOK LIKE MY KINDA GAL! ARE YOU DOING ANYTHING AFTER THE WEDDING?
WELL, YOU ARE KINDA CUTE FOR A CREEP.
CREEPER.
BACK OFF, CHUCKLES!
SHE'S TAKEN!

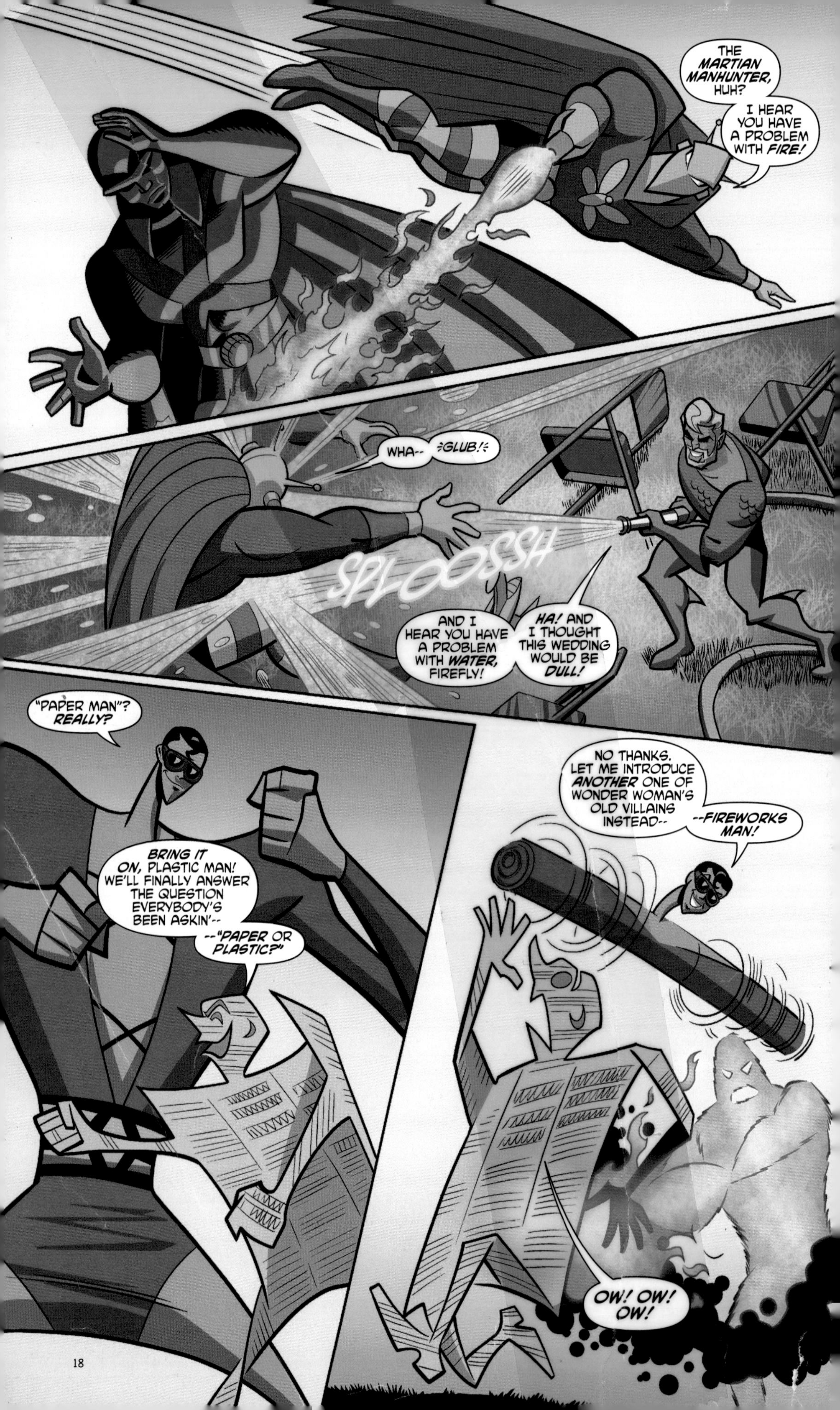
THE MARTIAN MANHUNTER, HUH?
I HEAR YOU HAVE A PROBLEM WITH FIRE!
WHA-- GLUB!
SPLOOSSH
AND I HEAR YOU HAVE A PROBLEM WITH WATER, FIREFLY!
HA! AND I THOUGHT THIS WEDDING WOULD BE DULL!
"PAPER MAN"? REALLY?
BRING IT ON, PLASTIC MAN! WE'LL FINALLY ANSWER THE QUESTION EVERYBODY'S BEEN ASKIN'--
--"PAPER OR PLASTIC?"
NO THANKS. LET ME INTRODUCE ANOTHER ONE OF WONDER WOMAN'S OLD VILLAINS INSTEAD--
--FIREWORKS MAN!
OW! OW! OW!

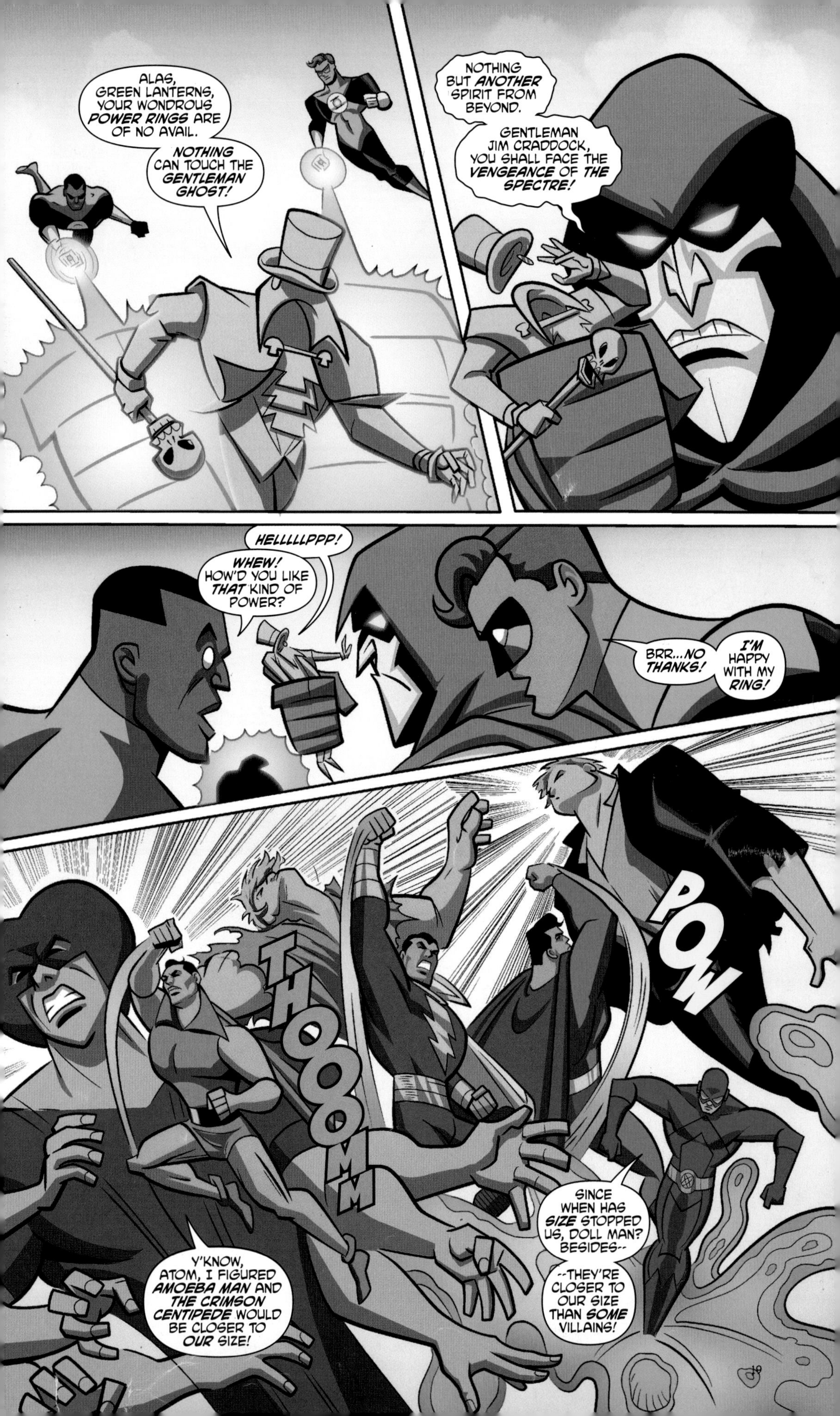
ALAS, GREEN LANTERNS, YOUR WONDROUS POWER RINGS ARE OF NO AVAIL.
NOTHING CAN TOUCH THE GENTLEMAN GHOST!
NOTHING BUT ANOTHER SPIRIT FROM BEYOND.
GENTLEMAN JIM CRADDOCK, YOU SHALL FACE THE VENGEANCE OF THE SPECTRE!
HELLLLLLPPP!
WHEW! HOW'D YOU LIKE THAT KIND OF POWER?
BRR...NO THANKS!
I'M HAPPY WITH MY RING!
POW
THOOOMMM
Y'KNOW, ATOM, I FIGURED AMOEBA MAN AND THE CRIMSON CENTIPEDE WOULD BE CLOSER TO OUR SIZE!
SINCE WHEN HAS SIZE STOPPED US, DOLL MAN? BESIDES--
--THEY'RE CLOSER TO OUR SIZE THAN SOME VILLAINS!

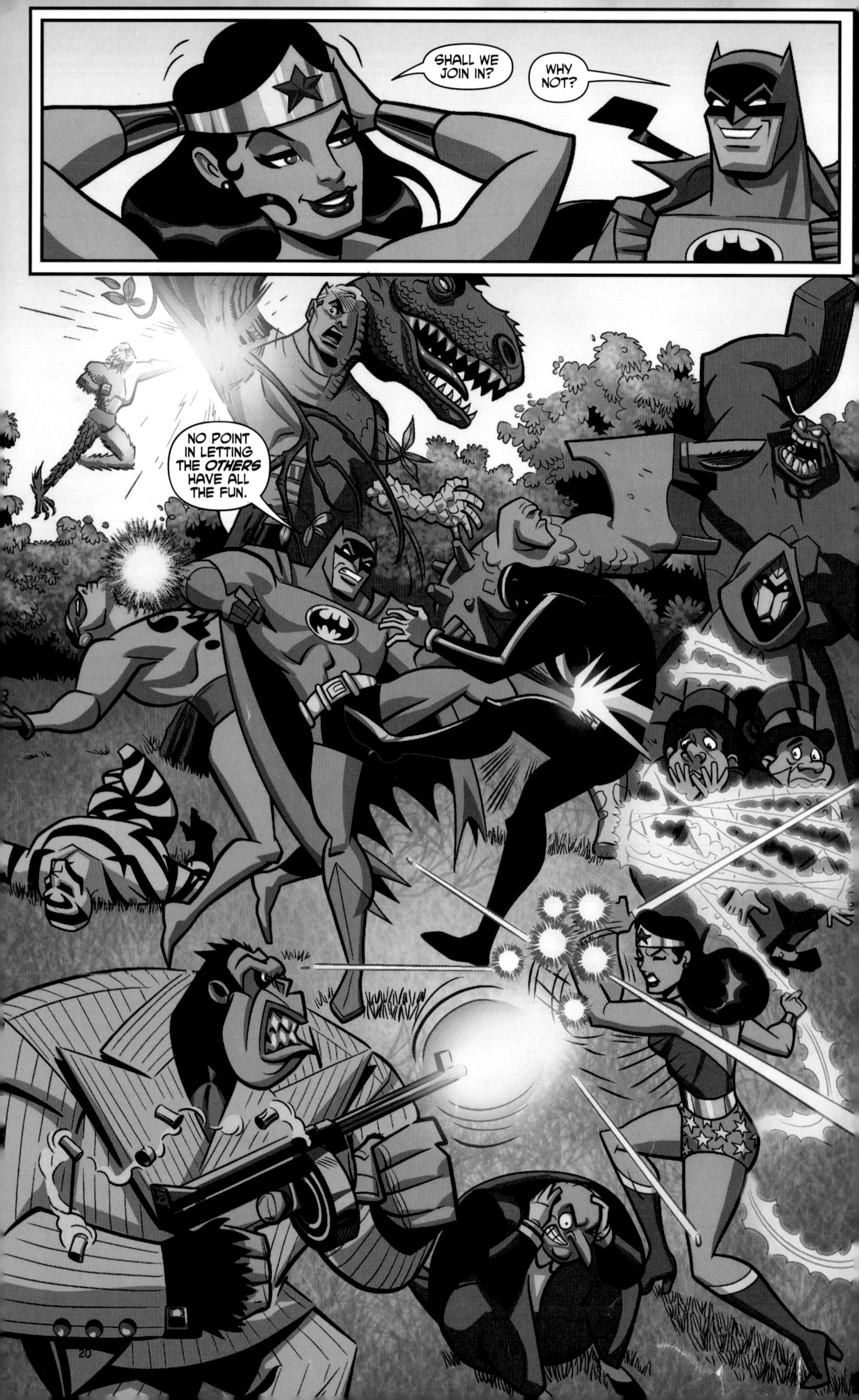

SHALL WE JOIN IN?
WHY NOT?
NO POINT IN LETTING THE *OTHERS* HAVE ALL THE FUN.

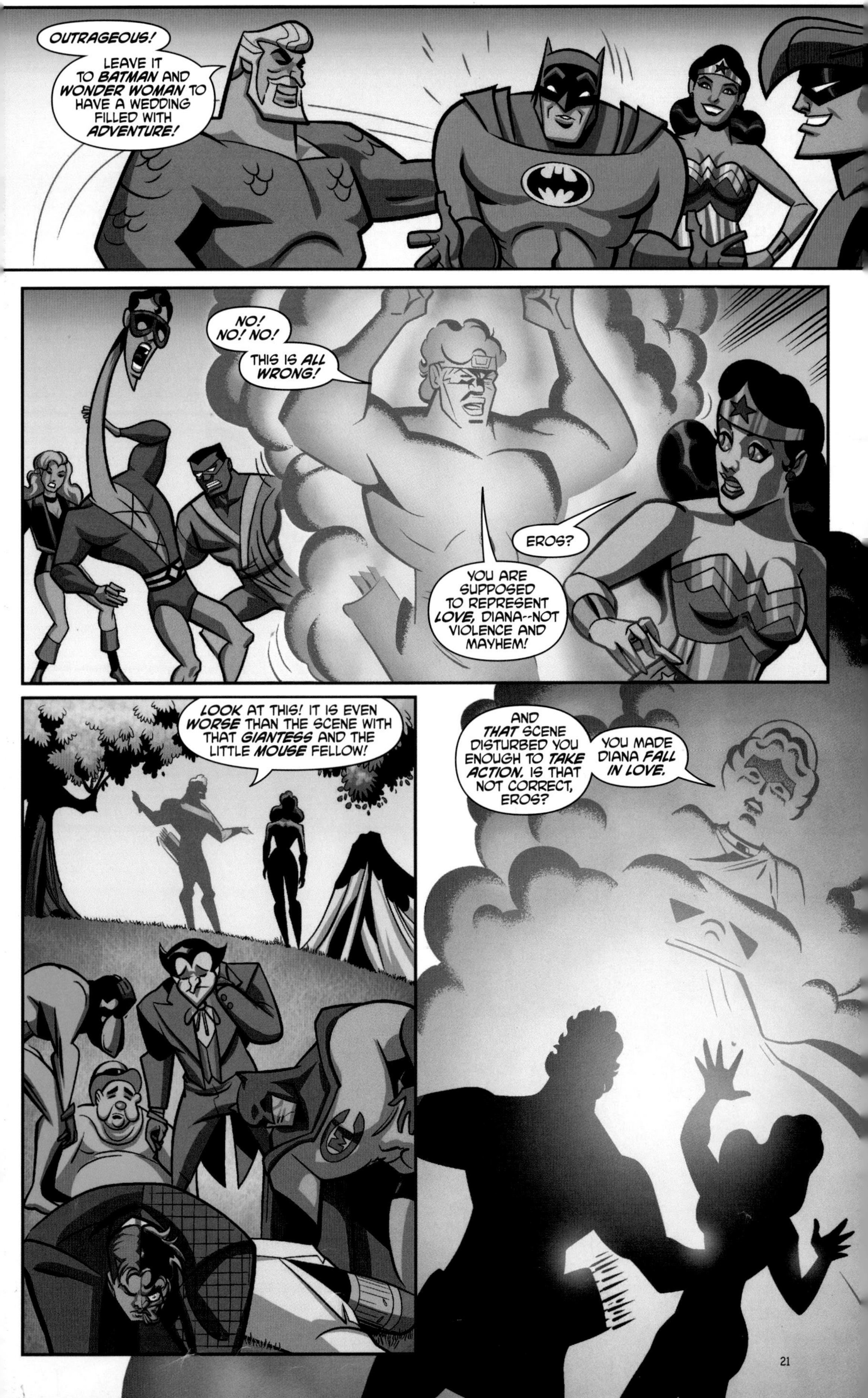
OUTRAGEOUS!
LEAVE IT TO BATMAN AND WONDER WOMAN TO HAVE A WEDDING FILLED WITH ADVENTURE!
NO! NO! NO!
THIS IS ALL WRONG!
EROS?
YOU ARE SUPPOSED TO REPRESENT LOVE, DIANA--NOT VIOLENCE AND MAYHEM!
LOOK AT THIS! IT IS EVEN WORSE THAN THE SCENE WITH THAT GIANTESS AND THE LITTLE MOUSE FELLOW!
YOU MADE DIANA FALL IN LOVE.
AND THAT SCENE DISTURBED YOU ENOUGH TO TAKE ACTION. IS THAT NOT CORRECT, EROS?

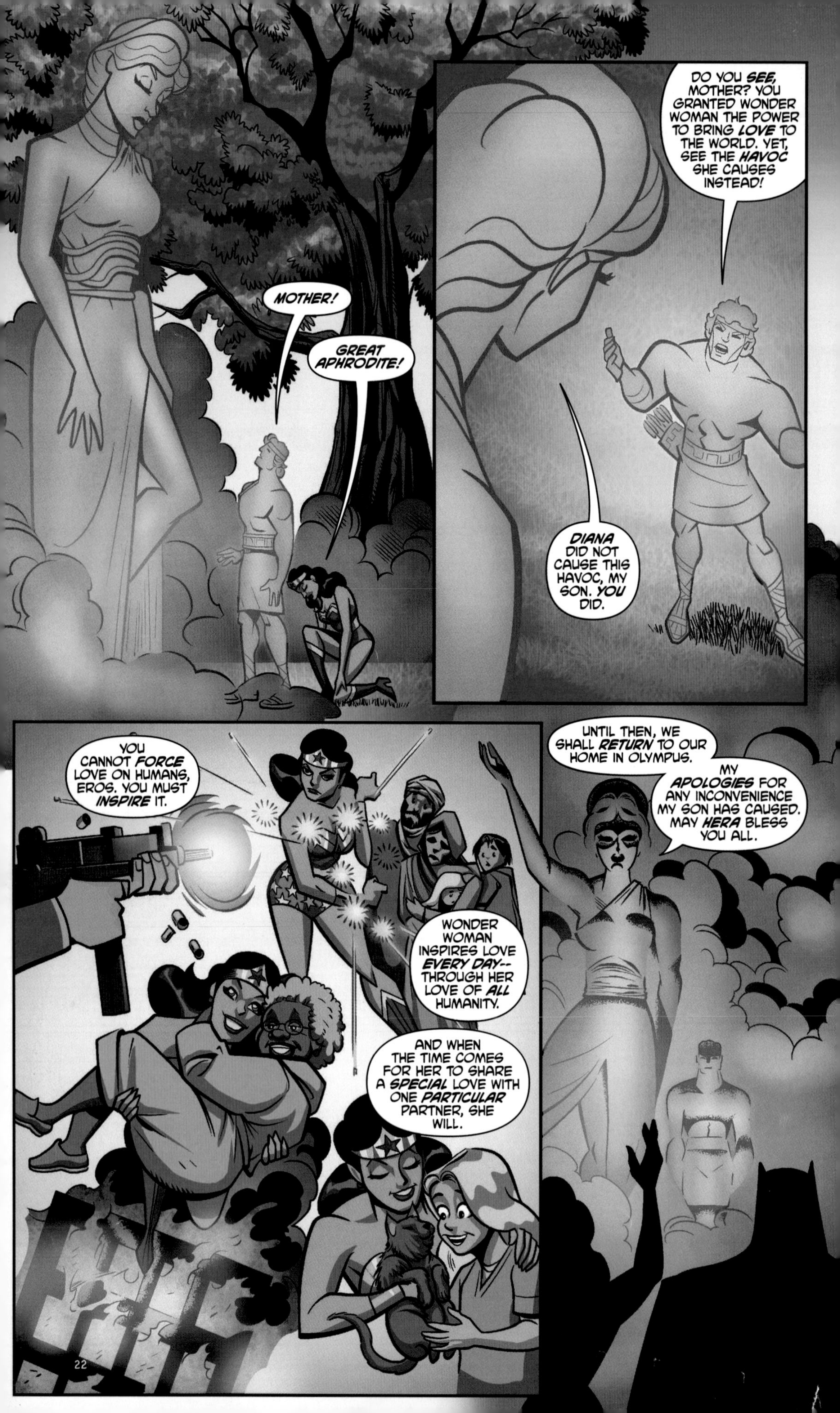
MOTHER!
GREAT APHRODITE!
DO YOU SEE, MOTHER? YOU GRANTED WONDER WOMAN THE POWER TO BRING LOVE TO THE WORLD. YET, SEE THE HAVOC SHE CAUSES INSTEAD!
DIANA DID NOT CAUSE THIS HAVOC, MY SON. YOU DID.
YOU CANNOT FORCE LOVE ON HUMANS, EROS. YOU MUST INSPIRE IT.
WONDER WOMAN INSPIRES LOVE EVERY DAY-- THROUGH HER LOVE OF ALL HUMANITY.
AND WHEN THE TIME COMES FOR HER TO SHARE A SPECIAL LOVE WITH ONE PARTICULAR PARTNER, SHE WILL.
UNTIL THEN, WE SHALL RETURN TO OUR HOME IN OLYMPUS.
MY APOLOGIES FOR ANY INCONVENIENCE MY SON HAS CAUSED. MAY HERA BLESS YOU ALL.

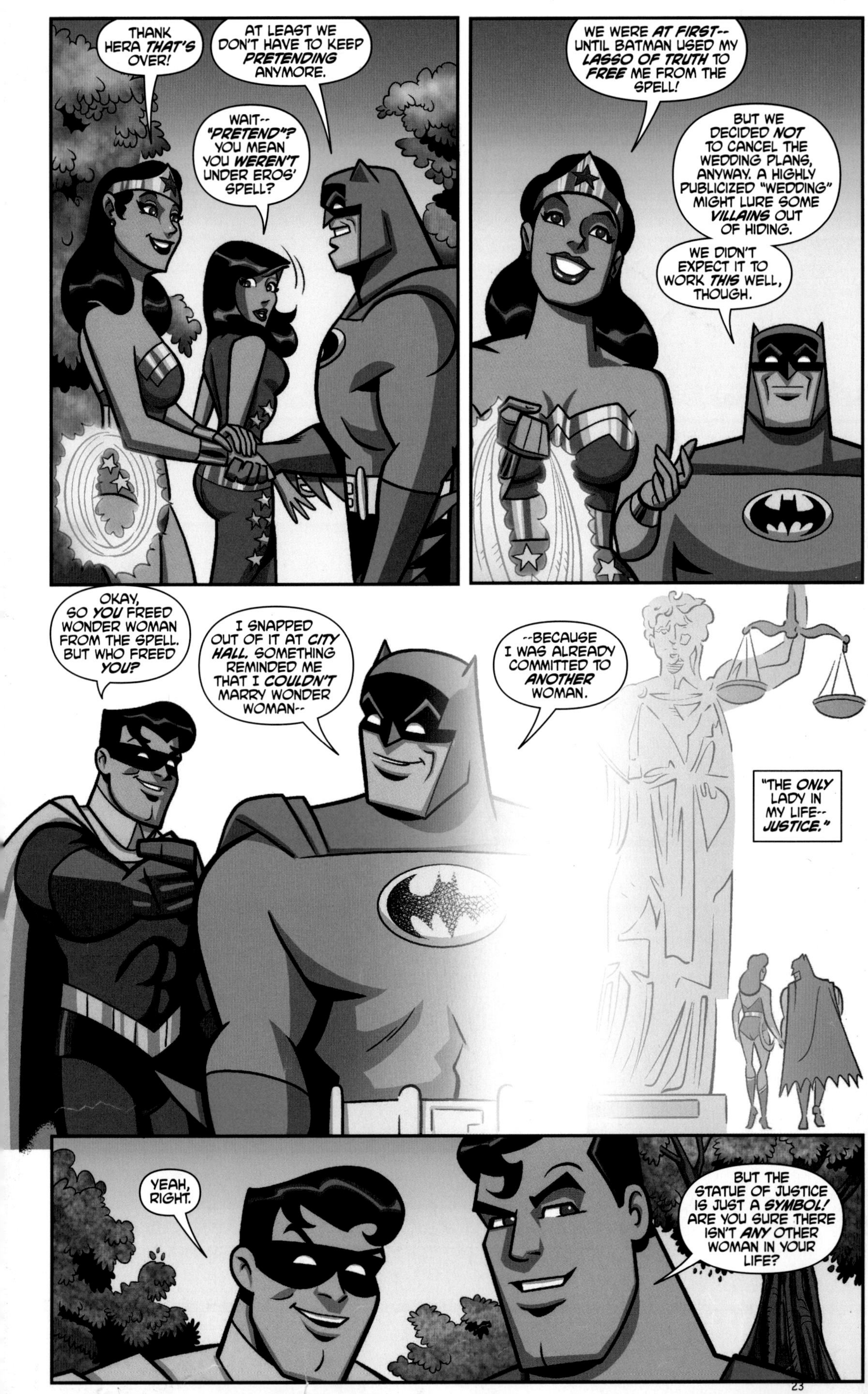
THANK HERA THAT'S OVER!
AT LEAST WE DON'T HAVE TO KEEP PRETENDING ANYMORE.
WAIT-- "PRETEND"? YOU MEAN YOU WEREN'T UNDER EROS' SPELL?
WE WERE AT FIRST-- UNTIL BATMAN USED MY LASSO OF TRUTH TO FREE ME FROM THE SPELL!
BUT WE DECIDED NOT TO CANCEL THE WEDDING PLANS, ANYWAY. A HIGHLY PUBLICIZED "WEDDING" MIGHT LURE SOME VILLAINS OUT OF HIDING.
WE DIDN'T EXPECT IT TO WORK THIS WELL, THOUGH.
OKAY, SO YOU FREED WONDER WOMAN FROM THE SPELL. BUT WHO FREED YOU?
I SNAPPED OUT OF IT AT CITY HALL. SOMETHING REMINDED ME THAT I COULDN'T MARRY WONDER WOMAN--
--BECAUSE I WAS ALREADY COMMITTED TO ANOTHER WOMAN.
"THE ONLY LADY IN MY LIFE-- JUSTICE."
YEAH, RIGHT.
BUT THE STATUE OF JUSTICE IS JUST A SYMBOL! ARE YOU SURE THERE ISN'T ANY OTHER WOMAN IN YOUR LIFE?

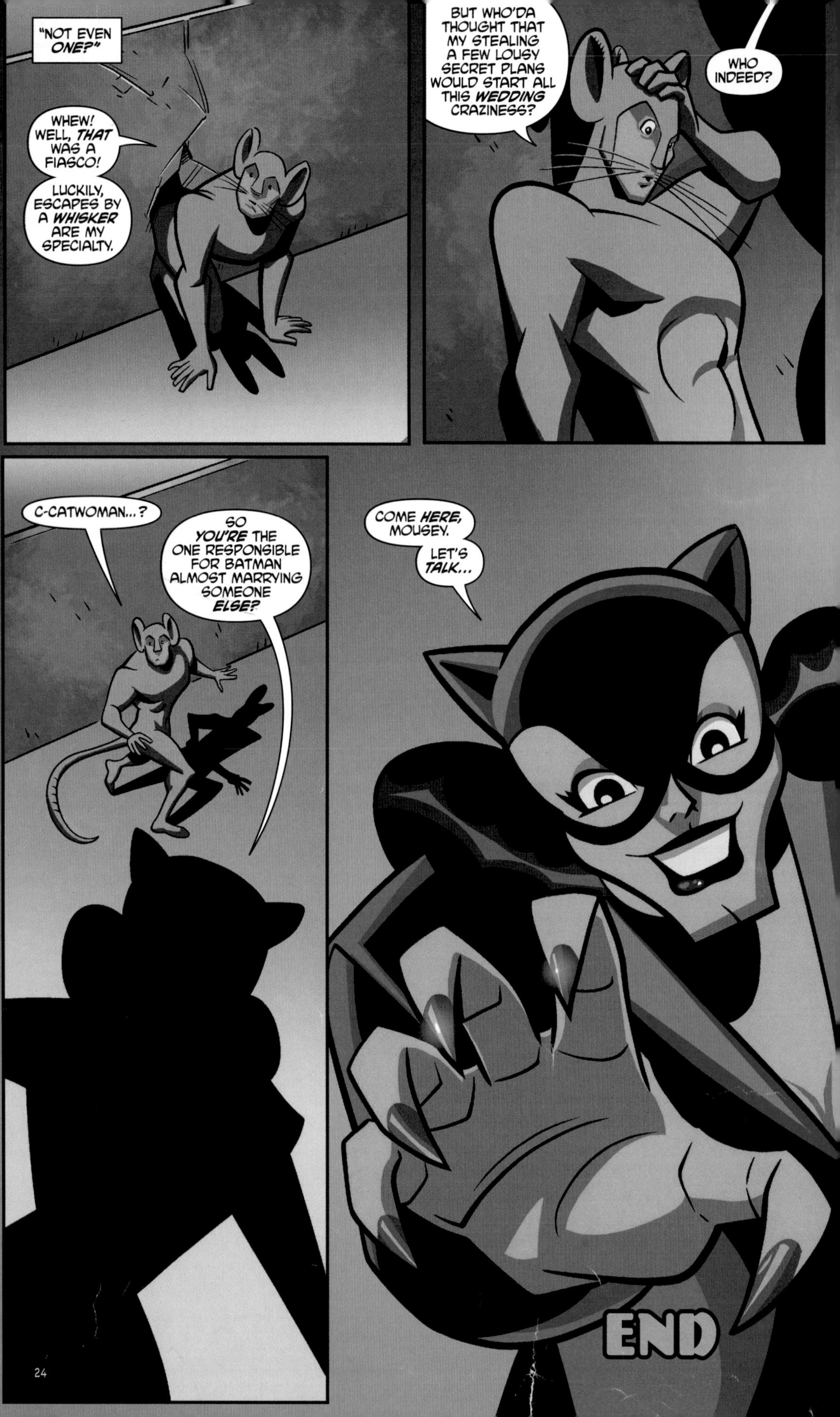
"NOT EVEN ONE?"
WHEW! WELL, THAT WAS A FIASCO!
LUCKILY, ESCAPES BY A WHISKER ARE MY SPECIALTY.
BUT WHO'DA THOUGHT THAT MY STEALING A FEW LOUSY SECRET PLANS WOULD START ALL THIS WEDDING CRAZINESS?
WHO INDEED?
C-CATWOMAN...?
SO YOU'RE THE ONE RESPONSIBLE FOR BATMAN ALMOST MARRYING SOMEONE ELSE?
COME HERE, MOUSEY.
LET'S TALK...
END

SHOLLY FISCH
WRITER

Bitten by a radioactive typewriter, Sholly Fisch has spent the wee hours writing books, comics, TV scripts, and online material for over 25 years. His comic book credits include more than 200 stories and features about characters such as Batman, Superman, Bugs Bunny, Daffy Duck, Spider-Man, and Ben 10. Currently, he writes stories for Action Comics every month, plus stories for Looney Tunes and Scooby-Doo. By day, Sholly is a mild-mannered developmental psychologist who helps to create educational TV shows, websites, and other media for kids.

RICK BURCHETT
PENCILLER

Rick Burchett has worked as a comics artist for over 25 years. He has received the comics industry's Eisner Award three times, Spain's Haxtur Award, and he has been nominated for England's Eagle Award. Rick lives with his wife and two sons near St. Louis, Missouri.

DAN DAVIS
INKER

Dan Davis has illustrated the Garfield comic series as well as books for Warner Bros. and DC Comics. He has brought a variety of comic book characters to life, including Batman and the rest of the Super Friends! In 2012, Dan was nominated for an Eisner Award for the Batman: The Brave and the Bold series. He currently resides in Gotham City.

GLOSSARY

accursed [ah-KERST]--being under a curse or detestable

assassin [uh-SAS-in]--a person who kills another person

avail [uh-VAYL]--to be of use or help

espionage [ES-pee-uh-nahzh]--the act of spying

exploits [EK-sploits]--brave or exciting actions

fiasco [fee-AS-koh]--a complete failure

inconvenience [in-kuhn-VEEN-yuhnss]--something that causes trouble

industrial [in-DUHSS-tree-uhl]--of or having to do with factories and making things in large quantities

lousy [LOU-zee]--really bad

nuisances [NOO-suhnss-ez]--things or people that are annoying or cause problems

spectre [SPEK-tur]--a ghost

vengeance [VEN-juhnss]--action you take to pay someone back for harm that she or he has done to you or someone you care about

VISUAL QUESTIONS & PROMPTS

1. How does the artist help us figure out that Giganta and Mouse Man are very different sizes?

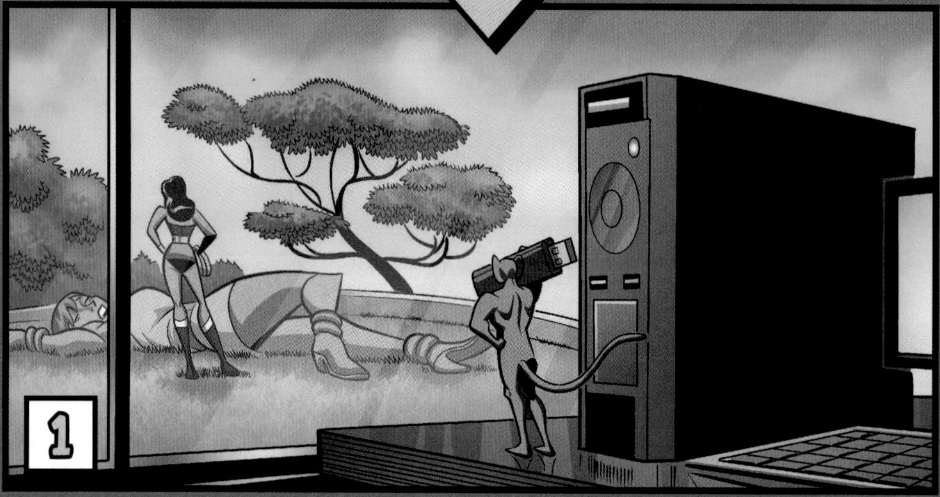

2. Who is speaking in this panel? Is there a different way the artist could have depicted this scene?

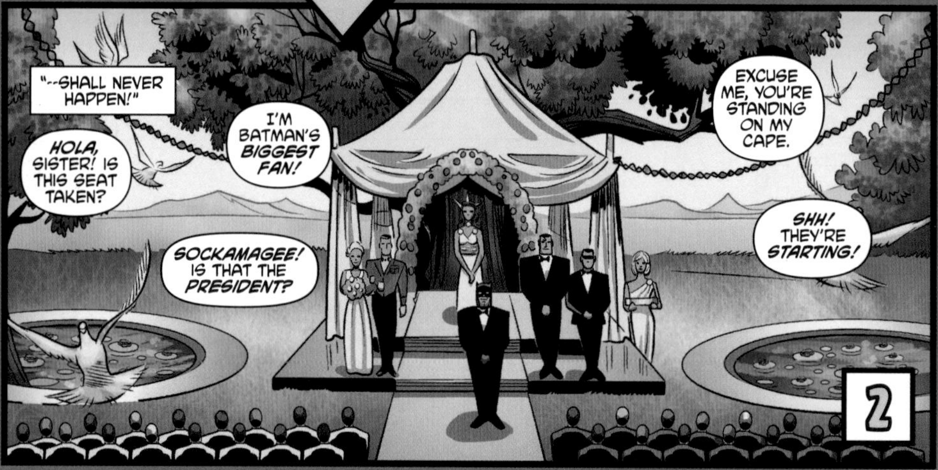
"--SHALL NEVER HAPPEN!"
HOLA, SISTER! IS THIS SEAT TAKEN?
I'M BATMAN'S BIGGEST FAN!
SOCKAMAGEE! IS THAT THE PRESIDENT?
EXCUSE ME, YOU'RE STANDING ON MY CAPE.
SHH! THEY'RE STARTING!
2

3. Artists have many different techniques they use to show that something is in motion. What are some of the ways the art shows that motion is occurring in this panel?

4. At the end of the story, Batman explains that he and Wonder Woman had been pretending they were in love. Knowing now that Batman used the Lasso of Truth to free Wonder Woman from the curse, go back and read the story again. Do you notice anything about the text or art that you didn't notice the first time?

READ THEM ALL!

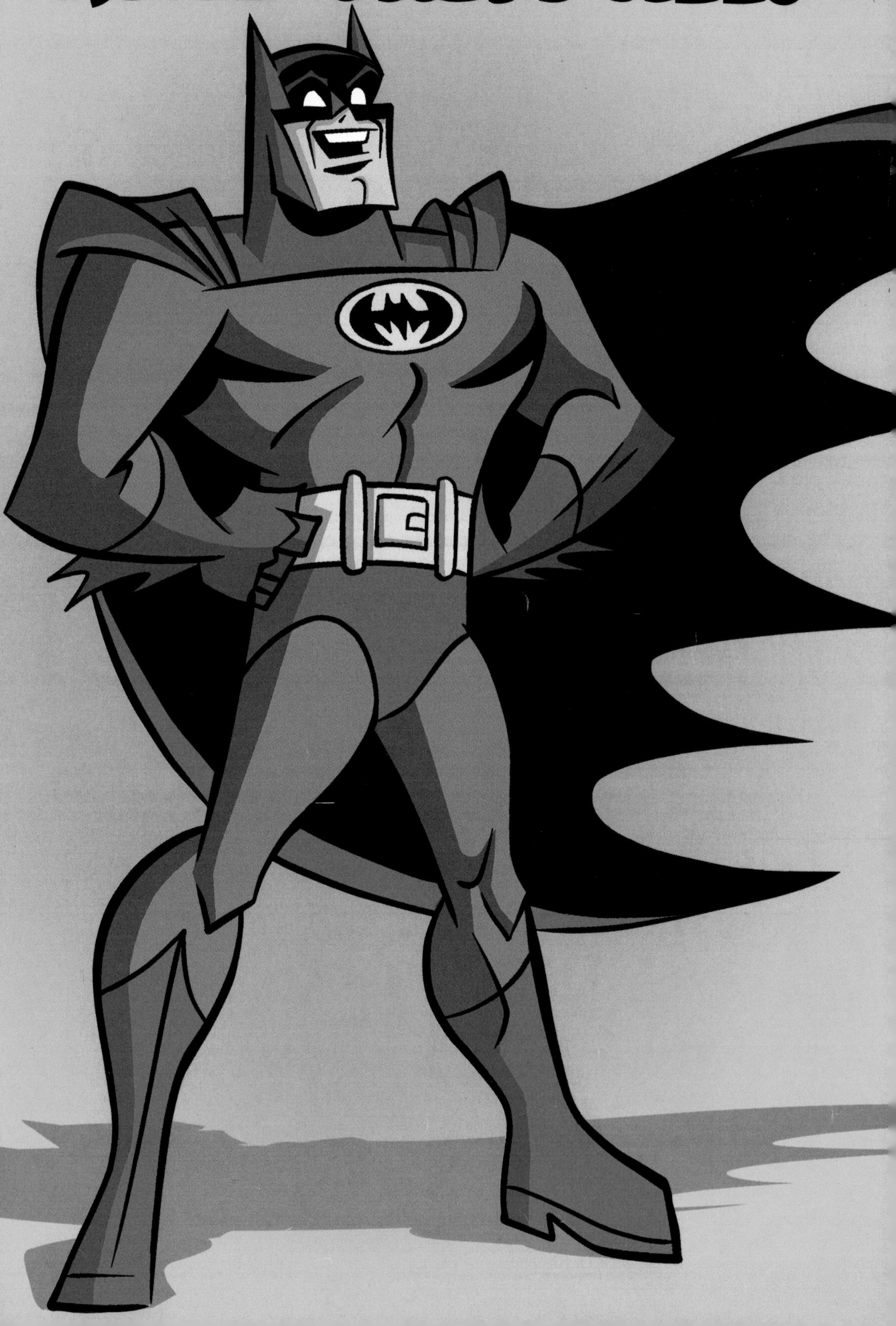

THE ALL NEW!
BATMAN
THE BRAVE AND THE BOLD

THE ALL NEW!
BATMAN
THE BRAVE AND THE BOLD
BOTTLE OF THE PLANETS
FISCH
BURCHETT
DAVIS

THE ALL NEW!
BATMAN
THE BRAVE AND THE BOLD
THAT HOLIDAY FEELING
FISCH
BURCHETT
DAVIS

THE ALL NEW!
BATMAN
THE BRAVE AND THE BOLD
THROUGH THE LOOKING GLASS
FISCH
BURCHETT
DAVIS

THE ALL NEW!
BATMAN
THE BRAVE AND THE BOLD
FISCH
BURCHETT
DAVIS
THE BRIDE AND THE BOLD

THE ALL NEW!
BATMAN
THE BRAVE AND THE BOLD
FISCH
BURCHETT
DAVIS
MANHANDLED BY MANHUNTERS!

THE ALL NEW!
BATMAN
THE BRAVE AND THE BOLD
FISCH
BURCHETT
DAVIS
CLOBBERED BY CLAYFACE!

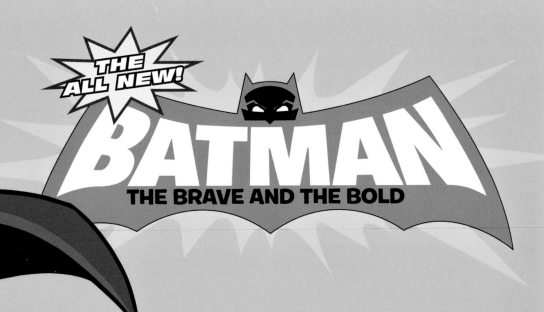

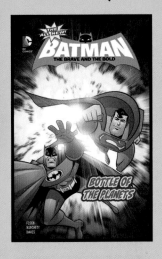

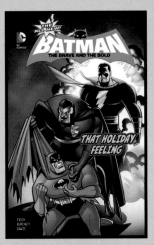

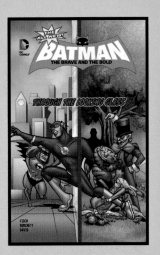

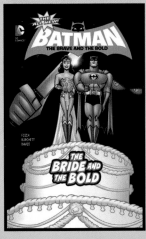

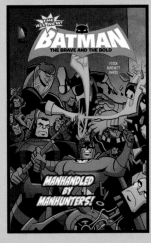

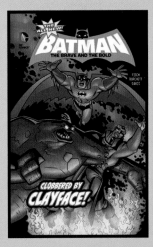

THE ALL NEW!

BATMAN

THE BRAVE AND THE BOLD

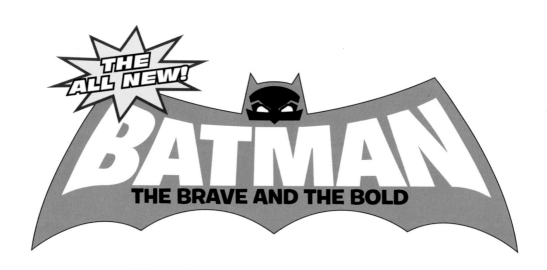